Percy Addleshaw, Roden Berkeley Wriothesley Noel

Selected Poems from the Works of the Hon. Roden Noel

Percy Addleshaw, Roden Berkeley Wriothesley Noel

Selected Poems from the Works of the Hon. Roden Noel

ISBN/EAN: 9783337398071

Printed in Europe, USA, Canada, Australia, Japan

Cover: Foto ©Andreas Hilbeck / pixelio.de

More available books at **www.hansebooks.com**

Selected Poems

From the Works of the Hon. Roden Noel with a Biographical and Critical Essay by Percy Addleshaw

WITH TWO PORTRAITS

London: Elkin Mathews
MDCCCXCVII

CONTENTS

CONTENTS

ILLUSTRATIONS

PREFACE

It is related of Christian that as he drew near to the House Beautiful "he entered into a very narrow passage .... and looking very narrowly before him as he went, he espied two lions in the way." Fortunately, as he pondered the advisability of retreating, he was reassured by Watchful crying out that the beasts were chained. I venture on the task of writing a preface to this collection of lyrics with feelings much the same as Christian's when the supposed danger first threatened him; but I know the two lions that eye my path are neither chained nor easily avoided. To speak plainly, it is over difficult to write concerning the work of a friend in such a manner as to be at once critical and just. There is for instance a temptation to overpraise, especially if the work noticed lack its full share of popularity. And it often happens that readers led on by the critic's enthusiasm are apt to become disgusted when the high hopes raised are not realized, to ignore real merit if it seem to fall short of the most exalted standard. Thus is a grave injustice done to him and them. But if this error be avoided there is yet another and more fatal one. The attempt to be sternly moderate, to allow all objections more than their due weight, may perhaps lead students to draw the conclusion that the poet or essayist is after all of no great importance. Thus again, and this time more seriously, because more permanently, is a great injustice done to him and them. I do not pretend to have avoided the difficulties that I have so keenly feared. Sins of omission and commission are mine; but I have striven zealously and can only hope, now, that I have been in some measure successful.

For Roden Noel was a man to whom I owed much, a man whom no one could meet without being in some degree his debtor. The dignity, courtesy, and charm of his manner were delightful and unusual; his conversation was always interesting, learned, and thoughtful, yet never dogmatic or patronising. In a word he was the best of teachers because he was the most gentle and appreciative of listeners. His faults were those of a child, perhaps a spoilt child, but the nobility of his character made it an easy matter to forgive the defects, such as they were. Indeed, they were often only a cause for amusement among his friends, and Noel himself had the spirit to join in and encourage the laughter. Though his writings are surprisingly destitute of humour, his talk was sparkling enough, and he could tell an anecdote with real dramatic effect. As a reader too, he had a strange power over his hearers. His was the Siddons tradition, and through Lord Gainsborough he had caught the "great" style as a reciter of verse. These early lessons in reading from his father had an effect on his own work. He tested its rhythm by its speaking qualities and would read a poem aloud several times, noting where the voice failed to sustain the music designed, and altering those defects his ear detected in the spoken sounds. He could move a large audience by the recitation of a few lines of verse in a way many an experienced actor might envy. I shall not readily forget hearing him read one summer night "Wild Love on the Sea", a poem written while he was the guest of my brother and myself at a tiny cottage on the south coast of Cornwall. His voice seemed to have caught the very thunder and hiss of the waves that we heard dashing on the rocks below the cliffs. Even now, looking at the printed page, I can still hear him declaiming the triumphant boast of the demon-lover:

"Ho, with storm to the windward, and breakers to lee,
  They go swimming with Death who go swimming with me."

Much of Noel's poetry may have a magic for me, and others of his friends, that it can never possess for those who were strangers to the man himself. What may seem rugged, uncouth, to them is melodious, significant, to us who still hear in many a stanza the wonderful music of that voice now, alas, silent.

Roden Berkeley Wriothesley Noel was the third

son of the Earl of Gainsborough. His mother was a daughter of the Earl of Roden, an ardent Protestant, and Head of the Orange-men in Ireland. He was born in 1834 and was educated at Harrow and Trinity, Cambridge, graduating M.A. 1858. He was intended for the church and it was expected that he would succeed to a living in the family gift. On leaving the University he still acceded to this plan. But the two years he spent in Egypt and Palestine turned his thoughts in other directions, and, greatly to the regret of his family, he abandoned all idea of taking holy orders. While lying dangerously ill at Beyrout, he was nursed by Madame de Broë, whose daughter he afterwards married. It was necessary to do something for a living, and for a time he worked at a business in the city. As a business man he was ludicrously incapable, lacking both the training and qualifications that command success. By the influence of his mother, who was lady-in-waiting to the Queen from the time of Her Majesty's accession till 1873, he became a groom of the Privy Chamber, an office he held for some years. But conscientious scru-

ples again came between him and his worldly
comfort, his leanings towards radical and, later
on, even socialistic teachings grew more pronounced.
Though his reverent affection for, and loyalty to,
the Queen never wavered, he felt that he must
resign. Noel was a man, though, who faced difficulties with courage, swerved not at all from
that which to him was right and honourable. For
the rest his days were passed quietly, unevent-
fully, in England, Italy, and the Riviera. Latterly
he lived at Brighton. The real events of his
life, as he would have considered them, were his
gradual changes of opinion on religious and socialistic questions, his literary work, and the weaning
of himself from prejudices, the inevitable outcome
of his aristocratic training and position. This last
was a hard and often bitter task, as he frequently
confessed.

His writings were in great part a commentary
on his own life. He did not believe in simulating
emotions, inventing experiences in order that he
might compose elegant or passionate verses about
them. He had a horror of "merely got up subjects". Although delighting in a purely intellec-

tual life, he often declared that " to live is above writing about it ". He was conscious of the dangers that threatened in the studies he ardently pursued. Browning's work suffered, as he confessed, owing to the " omnivorous learning " of the poet of " Pippa ": a learning not always " subordinate to poetic ends ". Unfortunately he entangled himself in a similar snare more than once, so that a good deal of his poetry was strangled at its birth. It might have been expected that his two years in the East would have given him a clearer utterance as well as a larger vocabulary. His oriental poems, it is true, are richly coloured, full of descriptions accurate and brilliant. One of their most ardent admirers was Tennyson, who declared of " Azrael " that it was " very lovely " and wrote of the " Vision of the Desert," " It is one of the finest things I have ever read." Tennyson sent for Noel after he had read these eastern poems, and gave the younger writer much advice and encouragement. " You don't mind my saying all this ? " he asked at the end of the interview—" I should not do it if I did not think it worth while. Coleridge did exactly the same for me when I

B   xvii

was beginning." Years after, not long before his
death, Tennyson wrote "you are no minor poet . . .
Your book is full of true poetry, not concentration
enough perhaps." The fault thus noted by the
greater poet was certainly fostered by Noel's eastern
voyages.

The splendour of the East seemed to demand
a magnificence of language which Noel endeavoured
to attain by means not altogether fortunate. A
long review of *Beatrice* in the Pall Mall Gazette
of Feb. 9th 1869, while praising cordially such
poems as "Ganymede" and "Palmyra", which are
ranked among the highest poetry, lays due stress
on the danger he ran from his "agglutinative use
of epithets." The criticism was deserved, it was
only in his very latest work that he managed to
shake off the trick. But on the other hand Noel
gained much by his travels. Both thought and
vocabulary were perceptibly enlarged. It needed
just this contact with men of other creeds, this
sight of other lands and customs to destroy the
narrow Calvinistic creed that would have crushed,
inevitably, much of his best poetry; would have
condemned and stifled the inspiration that gave

birth to " Mancheres" or " The Water-Nymph and the Boy." What the intellectual life at Cambridge had failed to do, his wanderings accomplished, and the result was a great literary gain, though from a spiritual aspect the change for the better was not quite so evident at first. Here it is enough to show that for good or evil his eastern experiences gave him a direct impetus, a peculiar manner, which he never got rid of, nor indeed wished to get rid of. Henceforth the "mere joy of living" was a real healthy delight to him. The first step towards true happiness and knowledge was thus gained: the rest was to come later.

From 1867 to 1871 Noel was a groom of the Privy Chamber, and was probably better off, materially, than at any time of his life. His duties, if not altogether to his taste, even from the first, were light, and left him plenty of time for literary work. The letters he wrote at this period were full of discussions on books, philosophies, and political events. Gradually he became more and more advanced in his political opinions. The Franco-German war, the terrible events in Paris that followed it, rivetted his attention. As

one who had known the Emperor he was interested
in the fortunes of the third Napoleon, but it was
the sufferings of the mob that called most for
his sympathy. One result of his study was to
spur him to a minute inspection of the London
streets; the terrible condition of the poor preyed
heavily on his mind. He deserted Palmyra to
discover Whitechapel. Pity for the misery that
jogged elbows with so much useless luxury, in-
dignation at the frequent injustices made in the
name of a sham freedom, stirred his wrath. He
published at this time *The Red Flag*, a bitter
satire with the refrain :

"There is Peace in London."

From this period his interest on the toiling
masses and *above all in the children*, became one
of the chief concerns of his life. Henceforth
much of his poetry is indignant satire or tender
appealings for the oppressed poor. The great
lesson he learned from the war may be summed
up in his grim commentary on England's boasted
happiness and freedom.

"The lonely toiler, gasping for some air,
Listens in shadowy poison of the stair,

Listens, a wounded beast within his lair

. . . . And there is Peace in London."

Now and henceforth the sorrows and burdens
of the poor cast a great shadow over his own
life, as all who knew him can testify. The proper,
though necessarily rather selfish, impulse to earn
a name for himself, common to all young writers,
was changed into the desire to use what powers
he had at his command for the furtherance of
the well-being of those unfortunates on whom the
cruelty of the world told most terribly. Nor was
he content to write; he worked zealously to ad-
vance his ends, often beyond his strength. Never
a rich man, he could give little but his labour,
and that he gave willingly. The result was not
altogether good for his literary work, because he
subjugated his art too severely to his moral code.
He gave up, for example, a long cherished plan
of writing " A Triumph of Bacchus," as ill-befitting
his new mission. No day now passed without
the pushing forward of some scheme for the
benefit of others. The tone and manner of his
work reflected his fierce and militant sympathy.
His writing was never divorced from his every-

day life; the building of a cabman's shelter at Penge, the carrying of toys to a children's hospital, the founding of a branch of the S.P.C.A. at San Remo, were as important as the completion of a poem or essay. His written work indeed was the record of the life he tried bravely with all his strength to live. Once in a letter to a friend he wrote " Definite vision and intense emotion seem to me the first requisites of a poet." He had seized now his definite vision ; the intense emotion told on his health. He wrote with his life's blood, and, whatever its faults, work so written has a great value. He answered, with anger even, a correspondent who had suggested that "A Poor People's Christmas" could not, because of its subject matter, be considered poetry. A curious result of his newly-stirred sympathies was the forgetting, or wilful ignoring, of much of his nicely reasoned philosophy. Whereas he had been wont to state reasons and draw vague conclusions, he now stuck to facts and declared them to be a disgrace to the national character, evils that ruined the nation's health. If his own remedies were not faultless his personal endeavours

were honest, unwearied, unselfish: his own life
was the nobler for his devotion and zeal. It did
not occur to him that some of the misery in the
world was the direct result of folly and crime.
He chose rather, to blame our modern civilization
for all the squalor he saw around him; the greed
of kings and nobles, the avarice, folly and self-
ishness of society in general. So he launched a
series of satirical poems, savage, courageous, terrible. He was determined that some one should
be whipped for the wrongs inflicted on the weak.
His abuse was indiscriminate, his invectives unjust.
Indeed, owing to their exceeding vehemence his
satires lost not a little of their force. He struck
always with a bludgeon, forgetting that the rapier
is the deadlier weapon. Yet one admires the
writer, though it is not at these moments one likes
him best. At the same time it is but justice to add
that he sometimes managed to slay his enemy with
admirable dexterity. If he could not emulate
Pope he proved more than once an apt pupil of
Dryden. Those in need of vigorous and terse
epigrams will find plenty to their hand in some
of Noel's stinging couplets. Once read they have

the burr-like quality of sticking. Very slight efforts of memory are required to bring them into play. This is a further, and unanswerable, sign that they possess real merit and distinction. What could be happier than this couplet on the doctrines of Malthus, Mill, and other economists, parodying that famous old panegyric on his own class?

> "Perish the human race to verify
> Our pet political economy."

And though the Church of England has been busy setting her house in order these latter days, there is still some timely truth and a good deal of rough literary merit in these lines.

> "Now 'tis a Dean who, as he ambles by,
> Raises a question of church millinery,
> Or, in allusion to the squalid street,
> Observes that, howsoever God may mete
> The lot of each, all should be docile; which
> One may name 'Gospel according to the rich.'
> If there were no starvation for the mean,
> Supplies might fail us for a portly Dean."

Here it always seems to me we have an excellent commentary on Sidney Smith's assertion that

ours is a "country where poverty is infamous".
A doctrine firmly believed by most of us, and
one Noel was often at pains to combat. Of
course, however brilliant and poignant satire may
be, there is no form of literary expression that
dies more quickly. Notable exceptions may be
quoted readily enough, but I think my proposition
is practically unchallenged. Nor, indeed, could
we well expect any other fate for the majority
of poems that attack and quiz a state of things
that will be altered by time, a fashion that is
fleeting, an abuse remedied by age. So it is
that men of even rare ability, such as Churchill,
have now a plentiful lack of readers. One regrets,
now and again, that Noel wrote so much in this
form. The idea comes to us that he might
better have employed the time so spent in polish-
ing and strengthening his poems of philosophy,
nature and imagination.

I expect, though, that Noel's satires are the
proper complement of his tenderer verses in praise
of heroism, faith, and kindness among the humble.
The man who grows most angry at an abuse is
likely to proclaim a merit the more eagerly. He

who attacks an enemy without fear is ever the best lover and friend.

It was that he might more honourably attack the enemy that he had resigned his position at Court. Lady Gainsborough in vain endeavoured to dissuade him: and it hurt him keenly to distress the mother whom he loved so passionately. A weaker man would have hesitated, but his determination was fixed. He decided that it was his duty not only to direct his pen towards the nobler uses he dreamed of, but as he colloquially put it "to find most of the butter for his bread". Regrets, fortunately, he had none, he was content to risk being poorer if he could make others happier.

I well remember his telling me about the whole matter one hot day in August in Cornwall. We were resting near the cliffs looking over the blue sea he loved, and we could hear the waves dashing on the grim rocks below us. It was not many months before his death, and he had confessed already to certain signs that warned him he was near his end. Therefore he spoke solemnly but with full confidence in the rightness of his conduct and a little sorrowfully of unaccomplished things, blaming himself severely for many failures that to the less eager had seemed inevitable from the first. The very words he spoke to me are almost identical with a passage in a letter of his written to Professor Sidgwick in 1863. A man does not readily change the expression of an article of his faith. "Intellect is not the most divine element in my creed, it is love. Therefore Christ and not Goethe is the ideal of humanity, the point where the divine most fully saturates the human—i.e. the Son of God to whom we shall strive to be conformed. But to Him all that was human was sacred . . . . It is plain that if Goethism is right we should have a series of isolated, well-cultivated human units, only working for society where it is clearly seen to be to their interest, but self being the end of all. If Christ's spirit is right, Love and universal sympathy with all good would actuate each and unite each to all by an indissoluble bond . . . . That one may be fitted to be the instrument of good one must cultivate oneself. And one must have that genuine sympathy which prompts us to put ourselves in their position, to share their infirmities, put up with their imperfections, and oppose only their want of love."

Among all democrats the name of Roden Noel should be worthily esteemed. He gave up much that brings credit and comfort, to help such as needed help. Whether he always spoke and acted discreetly is a small matter: he had at any rate gained the right to speak and act. As he said of Livingstone, he too

"Lent a large heart to small perplexities
And simple tales of hourly human woe."

An almost Quixotic desire to destroy the world's evils grew stronger with each of his remaining twenty years. He had made no empty and high-sounding vow, he was not content with words of good courage. He tried by zealous work, often at useful objects scorned of the noisier philanthropist, to leave the world better than he found it. His intellectual studies were of the hardest. The list of books he read is enormous and strangely varied. So he soon realized, though probably tutored by his heart quite as much as by his head, that the only method of reclaiming the world with any prospect of permanent success was by protecting, educating, and caring for the children. He had long laboured actively among the children of the lower classes, had bidden successfully for their love. Now his pen was to work for them too with such skill and eloquence as he could command. His sympathy with all sufferers, his anxiety concerning the welfare of the elder poor did not diminish. Only he had come to half understand that the terrible curse weighing upon them could not be lifted by human hands. The little ones, "God's little ones", whom he once called, with an arrogance surely noble, "my little ones", seemed well within human power to aid. Therefore he ministered to them assiduously, visiting their hospitals and playgrounds, pleading for them in speech and poem. It is a curious fact that most of his child poems date from the time when he resigned his court appointment. Henceforth his tenderest ambition was to see his children's children,

"Play like a last dear dawn around his age".

There is about all his poems of child-life a

curiously bald simplicity, unconsciously almost humorous, yet pathetic despite, or may be because of the humour, that gives them a conspicuous value. Moreover in them the critic cannot dub the poet wayward and difficult to understand. Their charm once realized they remain with one always, not easy to forget; to some of us forgetfulness were not only difficult but impossible. One of the most haunting of these poems occurs in Book 3. of *A Modern Faust*. It strikes the note of his attitude towards the future of the world. He knew no pleasanter, cheerier sound than that of "the younger generation knocking at the door." The tenderness and gentleness, that endeared him to his friends, are emphasized in his prophecy that hereafter the children shall greet even the cruel "with forgiving kiss".

To a man of Noel's character and training, religion and philosophy concerned him greatly. Bred in the stern school of Calvin, even in his later years, when he cherished other and kindlier dogmas, he could still declare "I have never got over my Calvinistic education which taught me to disbelieve in "free-will", as it is usually defined by philosophers. "Man only becomes free when he realises his divine sonship and becomes an unerring law and impulse to himself." His love of children above all else brought him to a healthier attitude than that in which he was reared. He pinned his faith to the maxim that man must have a religion, and the uncompromising hostility to religion was the only reason, he said, that alienated his sympathies from the Commune. Yet he too lost his hold on any tangible faith, regarding Christ as one to be revered because of the beauty of his life, but never prayed to, as He had gone the way of all flesh. The misery he saw in the world was for a time a masterful argument, with him, against all creeds. But he returned to his belief in Christianity, led by the hand of a little dead child: out of evil came good, the great grief was, as he recognised at last, the great blessing. But his little son's death was a blow under which he staggered for long. Faithless, hopeless, believing that his " little Eric was put out altogether," he felt as if he were going mad. "For more than a year I cared for nothing, not literature, not even nature; yet Nature was something to me even then, I suppose, for I went alone to Sark and swam a great deal in the sea among the wonderful caves." During this weary year he turned again to the philosophers seeking comfort, and found it "unwittingly" in the New Testament. It was at this time he wrote the series of poems called *A Little Child's Monument*, his most enduring title to remembrance. The early poems are despairing, the latter gravely glad. There is in the volume none of that full flood of words, that often turgid eloquence, that involved meaning, noticeable in his other books. Each poem of the series is simple, poignant, eloquent. There are pages in it hard to read aloud with a steady voice, pages that hurt one with the anguish they portray: others that console and cause the unthinking to reflect. The style is stronger, because of its simplicity. The poems which had won the approval of Saint Beuve, with all their beauties, their descriptions of nature and arguments on philosophies and systems, lacked the moving sincerity of these memorial verses. It is possible, as an able critic has said, that their strange merit, their unique beauty "may easily miss us at first, but it is no less true that these qualities inevitably find us out at last, in virtue of the very straightness and sureness of their imaginative aim."

Naturally comparison was provoked with Tennyson's great memorial poem. Nor has *A Little Child's Monument*, save by a few, been ranked on a level with the elder poet's tribute to the dead. The comparison is not of my seeking, for comparisons are more often than not misleading. Nor does there seem any valid reason why they should have been compared. Beyond the fact that both are lamentations they have nothing in common. The grace, the ease, the subtle harmony of Tennyson were denied to Noel. But there is more of sincerity, a more spontaneous outpouring of grief in *A Little Child's Monument* than we find in the late laureate's work. Tennyson gives one the idea of having nursed his sorrow so assiduously that it became a positive luxury. He twisted his sentences, polished his lines, wove his graceful melodies with a dainty care repugnant to poignant grief.

Though we know how well Tennyson loved his friend, though we admire the beauty of his poem, we read it with dry eyes. We admire it for its exquisite fancies, its clever epithets and happy phrases: but as an expression of grief it fails to move us. On the other hand Noel's work truly voices his woe, and perchance for that very reason is at times almost inarticulate.

"Nature was something to me even then, I suppose". Clearly nature was much to him, more than she had ever been before. In no other poems of his are there finer descriptions of mountain, cloud, and sea: in no other poems so clear a perception of nature's mystery and laws. The frank gushing enthusiasm of early years that "rapture of strong youth's acclaim", gives place to a tender reverence for, a worshipful solemnity in the presence of, such a sight as

"Monte d'Oro,
His spirit robes far floating, a dim grey,
Sombre with forests, pallid with the moon,
His kingly crest snow-gleaming to the stars."

The religious side of Noel's character, always active, dominated in his later years all other

feelings and sentiments. He was at one with
Dr. Johnson in believing "that there must be
either a natural or a moral stupidity if one lives
in neglect of so very important a concern." He
could now look the world fully in the face, for-
tified by the new knowledge so hardly earned.
Of course how far poetry may be regarded as a
fit vehicle for philosophic and religious expression
is a moot point. But it cannot be shirked by
anyone trying to estimate the value of Noel's
output. Much of it indubitably suffers heavily.
There certainly ought to be an appearance of
spontaneity about poetry that is difficult of attain-
ment when the accurate reasoning of the logician
is attempted: both verse and logic are likely to
be of the poorest. But there is no doubt that
the deeper emotions and those profound truths
that cannot be argued about, only asserted and
felt, are fit subjects for poetry. Indeed poetry
alone should touch them. And I think that Noel
at his best understood this theory and accepted
it. There is not so much reasoning as affirmation
about the verities his study of the sea, the mountains, human nature, compelled him to proclaim.

It was with conclusions only that his later poems chiefly concerned themselves, he was content to reason in prose. And those conclusions he stated emphatically in that form which he conceived to be the highest and most enduring type of human speech. Concerning his philosophy and his poetry a wise and famous critic has written as follows: "The philosophy which distinguished Mr. Noel among his brother poets is better adapted, I think, to the medium of verse than prose exposition, and in *A Modern Faust* it reaches final expression. To characterise it by any single term is difficult. One might venture to call it uncompromising idealism. The Universe appears to Mr. Noel, as to Giordano Bruno, a God—penetrated unity. Nothing is real except spirit, and all is spirit. No one has felt the world-pain, the agony of sin, the cruel curse of evil more acutely. No pessimist, not Leopardi nor James Thomson, has depicted what men and women suffer, with such poignant realism, such tender sympathy. Unlike metaphysicians he deals with no mere abstractions. His grasp upon the concrete is even more remarkable than his habit of looking beyond and through the concrete to its substratum. In like manner his familiarity with speculative problems does not make him a mere visionary. The poet's eye for colour, shape, all things of sense, remains undimmed. To some tastes, indeed, his descriptions of natural joy, his appreciation of the voluptuous and gorgeous will appear extravagant... With the same keen sense of reality he feels the pure, the tender, the pathetic, the holy things of life; the heroism of brave men and martyrs, the sublime beauty of the loving, suffering Christ, the saintliness of noble women, the saving innocence of children. What constitutes this poet incommensurable is the extraordinary range of his sympathies, the justice of his touch upon so many diverse aspects of the outer and inner world, his combination of idealistic philosophy with artistic realism. It is easier to describe disorder than order in the world, when we are dealing, not with its physical laws but with its moral aspects. Yet the ethical value of Mr. Noel's work consists in the fact that he holds firmly to the belief that the everlasting No is illusion, the everlasting Yea reality; and he contrives by the force of his utterance to bring this belief home to our intelligence."

I can do no good by repeating, less ably, so complete and condensed a criticism of the ethical value of Noel's verse. There is a couplet at the close of one of the noblest poems Noel ever wrote which sums up in brief all his beliefs and hopes. It is the key-note of his later thoughts and speculations.

> "We lie within the tomb of our dead selves
> Waiting till one command us to arise."

But with the last line of the paragraph we come to the question of the poet's style, and it cannot be dismissed in the words " force of his utterance ". That he was an artist is unfortunately not nearly so certain. Matter is possibly more than manner, but manner is of vast importance; and many of his obscurities had been clear enough with defter handling. But however hard a man's work may be to grasp, however alien from our sympathies his methods, if he strive seriously and honestly he is entitled to careful study on the part of such as would play the critic. Refusing

to bestow the required attention is to put oneself out of court. This is surely common sense,
decently just; yet it is a rule often honoured in
the breach. To declare that Noel did not care
about style would be to betray oneself impetuous,
unobservant. He cared a great deal for, and sought
patiently after, adequate expression. True, the
result is often unsatisfactory, a nice ear is sometimes worried by painful discords. Noel never
quite understood the exact value of style; he
never tried to attain, because he never realized
the necessity of a style that should give his poems
distinction quite apart from what they professed
to say or teach. He made many sacrifices to
obtain a good manner as he understood it, but
he was always ignorant of the vital niceties that
rejoice the punctilious. So he was placed at a
disadvantage in addressing an audience that has
come to regard the mere phraseology as of
supreme importance. Though it cannot be said
that the bulk of modern verse, if inspired at all,
is greatly inspired, technically it is generally of
surprising merit. Delicate turns of expression,
intricate and fanciful measures, hitherto considered

a part of the Frenchman's heritage, have at last become native to ourselves. As a matter of fact verse-writers to-day are so full of dexterity that skill in metre and rhyme is no peculiar distinction. We have reason, doubtless, to congratulate ourselves. Have we not also something to regret? The average reader is not stirred to think by the average poet: neatness of touch has supplanted strength of imagination. And this, not because a fine feeling for words is an enemy to excellence of matter, but because the particular measures most favoured are fitted only for the most trivial themes. A triolet is a flippant answer to the riddle of human life. These newer fashions told hardly against a man of Noel's temperament. For him the matter was always greater than the manner. And he saw that the graces which lured the applause of the critics concealed a poverty of mind, a lack of knowledge. The poet should be not only minstrel but seer, in his eyes. "I cannot agree with you," he once wrote to Professor Sidgwick, "that sense and sentiment ought to be subordinate to sound in poetry." He always affirmed that there could be no high

thought, deep feeling, fine image, without more
or less adequate expression being simultaneously
born. It is true that he was too often content
with the "less adequate". A bad style, he contended, was an obtrusive, over elaborated style,
taking the first place instead of the second.
"You say it is not the thought but the expression that influences men. In part, yes—but you
need the substance more and you rarely get it."
The picture was to be as well framed as possible,
but only because the painting was worthy. He
deliberately contended that over-minuteness and
finish in cases where tenderness of human pathos
is concerned, where overwhelming scorn and
passion are portrayed, was a grave blunder. In
the process the feeling evaporated, the result
became shadowy, the image however lovely was
lifeless. He declared himself the pupil of Shake-
speare, Webster, Hugo, in style as in much else.
The plea is no bad one, it carries weight. How
far he was justified in his theories time alone
can show. It was not unimportant that he
justified himself, for it dowered his work with
the first and most permanent quality, sincerity.

PREFACE

I think he put too complete a confidence in his theories, and much that he wrote, otherwise admirable, will suffer and disappear in consequence. But whatever view one may take there is poetry of a good quality and a simple manner from his hand.

Apart from his poems for children, it is in those dealing with nature that his most enduring work will be found. He loved the hills and woods, the sea and the rivers with the love that only a man who understands nature thoroughly is permitted to acquire. For him there were silent voices in the world that the elect, and none but they, may hear. If, as their interpreter, he sometimes failed to convince, it is equally true that he often succeeded. After all is said he may fairly claim a place among our poets, for his great contemporaries hailed him gladly. Individual preference must contrive its own class lists. But he should pass honourably who won, through his verse, the praises of Saint Beuve, in France, of Tennyson and Browning at home. I, for one, am content to abide by their verdict, as Noel himself would have been.

This only remains to be said. When Noel

died a rare and beautiful spirit passed from among us. Those who loved the man loved his poems because they were his work. But it is inconceivable to us that others should not love them too. Some of his charm must surely hover around them, or we are greatly deceived. Believing this, the present volume has been compiled at the request of his family and friends. Ancient and honourable is our authority for believing that

"The words of a wise man's mouth are gracious."

PERCY ADDLESHAW

AT HIS GRAVE

IF death were an eternal sleep,
I would lay me down by him,
Never to wound more, nor to weep,
Nor grope aweary, maimed and dim,
Inflict no injury, no pain,
Nor ache with this dull doubt again!
While the birken shadows pass
O'er the marble and the grass,
I lean upon thy cross and weep;
Very sweet were sleep,
With ne'er a tear,
Nor hope nor fear!
If thou behold me from thy bowers
Smile on my offering of flowers,
And help me, dear!
Thou hast entered into life,
While we rave in mortal strife:
Love receive the offering

45

Of unworthy words I bring!
Lo! I lay them on thy tomb;
May they a little lighten gloom
Soothe an aching void and bless
In love's distress!

Thou should have laid me in my quiet
grave,
Sorrowing calm;
And I with folded palm.
But now, above thine own, behold I rave!
With all thy life before thee so to die,
Unseasonably!
"Whom the gods love die young;"
To that sweet saying then, I clung.

Ghastly Doubt and chilling Fear
The Wan Ages Quest is here,
Trembling Hope and faltering Faith,
Intent on what God whispereth.
It was thy leaving me that shook
Content in this deluding nook
Of rainbow life that seems upbuoyed
A moment in a rayless void;
So I sought for firmer ground,
And tell to others what I found.

I would embalm thee in my verse:
To loving souls it shall rehearse
Thy loveliness when I am cold,
And fragrant with it, may enfold
For other hearts in misery
Faint solace; words were sweet to me
From hearts who mourned what seemed to be
Dear, like thee;
These are thy swathings of rare spice
A golden shrine with gems of price,
A monument of my device.

LAMENT

I AM lying in the tomb, love,
Lying in the tomb,
Tho' I move within the gloom, love,
Breathe within the gloom!
Men deem life not fled, dear,
Deem my life not fled,
Tho' I with thee am dead, dear,
I with thee am dead,
O my little child!

What is the grey world, darling,
What is the grey world
Where the worm is curled, darling,
The deathworm is curled?
They tell me of the spring, dear!
Do I want the spring?
Will she waft upon her wing, dear,

LAMENT

The joy-pulse of her wing,
Thy songs, thy blossoming,
O my little child!

For the hallowing of thy smile, love,
The rainbow of thy smile,
Gleaming for a while, love,
Gleaming to beguile!
Replunged me in the cold, dear,
Leaves me in the cold,
And I feel so very old, dear,
Very, very old!

Would they put me out of pain, dear,
Out of all my pain,
Since I may not live again, dear,
Never live again!

I am lying in the grave, love,
In thy little grave,
Yet I hear the wind rave, love,
And the wild wave!
I would lie asleep, darling,
With thee lie asleep,
Unhearing the world weep, darling,
Little children weep!
O my little child!

DARK SPRING

Now the mavis and the merle
Lavish their full hearts in song;
Peach and almond boughs unfurl
White and purple bloom along
A blue and burning air,
All is very fair:
But ah! the silence and the sorrow!
I may not borrow
Any anodyne for grief
From the joy of flower or leaf,
No healing to allay my pain;
From the cool of air or rain;
Every sweet sound grew still,
Every fair colour pale,
When his life began to wane!
They may never live again!
A child's voice and visage will
Evermore about me fail;

And my weary feet will go
Labouring as in deep snow:
Though the year with glowing wine
Fill the living veins of vine,
While a faint moon hangs between
Broidery of a leafy screen;
And Night hear her Philomel,
While sweet lemon blossom breathes
And fair sun his falchion wreathes
With rich dependent golden fruit,
Or crimson roses at his foot,
All is desolate and mute!
Dark to-day and dark to-morrow!
Ah! the silence and the sorrow!

NIGHT AND MORNING

Suggested by Chopin's Funeral March

I

In the grey cathedral
In the aisles of twilight,
Wails an awful music,
Whelming my drowned spirit
Fathom deep in woe.
The hoar stone of ages
Palpitates disaster,
Breathes aware with sorrow,
Weighs me down to death!
All the immense wan spaces
Pregnant with dead faces,
Cold, carven forms arise!
And grey walls bring forth!
Vasty vans of darkness,
Swordsweeps of desolation,

Hound me to dim death!
Born from the deep ocean
Of sounding mystery,
In the ghostly forest
Of colossal pillars
Grows a dread procession:
Tramp! tramp! tramp!
Phantoms vast, sepulchral,
With dim downward eyes,
Move where yawns a dreary
Fathomless abyss.

What do they bear? They bear him,
My All, my Heart, my Heaven!
They let him fall therein!
Fall! fall! fall!
Fall ever in the abyss!
And my soul wails over,
Yearns to him in vain!
Cruel world! O cruel spirit
Of the world with ne'er a heart!
All in vain I moan imploring:
Sleep! sleep! sleep!

II

In the grey cathedral
Dawn red rays of morning,
And a low sweet music
Lifts me from the grave.
My dead pulses flutter,
As in spring the leaflet
Or young flower awaking
Wooed by the warm South . . .
. . . A calm saint on a pinnacle
Smiles in the day-dawn;
Monumental marble
With warm life-blood glows,
Sweet small singers warble
"Live! live! live!"
And lo! a rush of angels,
A cloud of spirits bright
From soft sun-rays of opal,
Woven to nests of light,

Among celestial branchings
Of the embowered height,
Bear me back my darling,
Smiling, rosed, alive,
Alive! alive! alive!
They only meant to scare me,
All was but in play;
The dismal shades were angels
From my Father's day;
Our Father knows why we must weep;
He wipes our tears away.
But if a hair might perish
From his sweet tendrilled head,
God would be the devil,
Love and Truth were dead,
Man a maniac mooning
A moment plausibly,
Joy an idiot fooling,
And life Death's leprosy!
    No! no! no!
An Eye rules the wild sea
Of human misery!

A TOMB AT PALMYRA

FULL twenty years! and still I seem to stand
As then, aloft in the tall tower tomb
So far within the expanse of Syrian sand,
Alone, where long, long ages in the gloom
Of yon stone shelves a human dust hath lain,
That once breathed, brooded, dared, hoped,
    hated, loved!
Awhile o'erwept, and worshipped with fond
    pain,
How stealthily the memory removed
From hearts who dreamed that never it
    could wane!
Later, the men who built the tomb dispersed,
Their conquerors were heedless of the dead:
Race following race, remembrance of the
    first,
Like some fair pageant of the cloud, is fled;
They, and the memory of them all erased,

Faint characters an idle mood hath traced
In sands of yonder ever-wandering waste.
The shelves are void; an alien spoiler soon
The dear embalmed remains hath lightly
    strewn
Upon these raving winds that roam the wild,
For ever to be scattered, whirled or piled
With dust that loved, scorned, knew not that
    they were,
For ever to be heaped and hounded there
With never-animate dust of the dun sea. . .
   . . . Anarchic spirits of the desert blast
Celebrate all the ruin of the past!
Shadowy Murder's dismal dialogue,
Conspiring, ere she leap to disembogue
Annihilating vials on my head,
Who dare to stand alive among the dead.
Carousals, wails from hollow hearts resound,
Long agony of maniac souls around,
Low moaning, shrieking, fading in a swound,
Thundering exultant through the rifted tomb,
And bearing down my heart with swoop
    of doom;
"Cease! cease from trouble! hope thou or
    despair;
"Wait but a little, thou too shalt be there!"

DEAD

I

WHERE the child's joy-carol
Rang sweeter than the spheres,
There, centre of deep silence,
Darkness and tears,
On his bed
The child lay dead.

II

There a man sat stolid,
Stupefied and cold
Save when the lamp's flicker
To poor love told
Some mocking lie
Of quivering eye,
Or lip that said,
"*He is not dead.*"

III

Weary Night went weeping,
Moaning long and low,
Till dim Dawn, awaking,
Found them so—
The heart that bled,
And his dim dead.

IV

"*Measure him for his coffin*,"
He heard a stranger say;
And then he broke to laughing,
"God! measure my poor clay,
And shut me in my coffin,
A soul gone grey!
For hope lies dead.
Life is fled."

THE KING AND THE PEASANT

WORLD-WIDE possessions, populous lands
The Monarch doth inherit,
And lordlier kingdoms he commands,
Fair realms within the spirit.
The monarch had a little son,
A child of five years old,
The loveliest earth e'er looked upon;
And he is lying cold.
The king is in the olive grove,
A hind sings in the tree;
Below, the infant of his love
Is babbling merrily.
The father beats the boughs, and while
Dark oval olives fly,
The boy with many a laugh and smile
Pursues them far and nigh.
Blue sea between the grey-green leaves
Twinkles, and the sun

Through them a playful chequer weaves
Over the little one.
The monarch gazes all unseen,
Tears burning his wan eyes;
Tenderly his love doth lean
To bless their Paradise,
As through black bars that foul the day,
And shut him out from joy:
Hear the world-envied monarch say,
" Perish my bauble crown, my toy,
All the science, all the sway,
Power to mould the world my way,
Persuade to beauty the dull clay!
Take all; but leave, ah! leave my boy,
Give me back my life, my joy!
This poor rude peasant I would be,
Yet dare not breathe the wish that he
Were as I am, a king of misery!"

"A MILK-WHITE BLOOMED ACACIA TREE"

A MILK-WHITE bloomed acacia tree,
　A flowery fair lawn,
Lark-song upsoaring from the lea,
　In a rosy dawn;
A little child who while he sings,
Gives light and joy to all, and song, and
　sunny wings!

The green acacia still blooms,
　And all the fairy flowers,
Song thrills the chorister's light plumes
　In blue celestial bowers;
Darkling I wander in the wild,
Looking for my little child;
I cannot hear his happy voice,
Bidding all the world be lovely and rejoice.

MOUNTAIN LYRIC

A MOUNTAIN spake to a sunny cloud,
" Whither, my child, away? "
" Father, the winds are calling loud
To fields of air for play!
Away! away!
Father, O father, solemn browed!
Fly thou with me for play!"
Nestled half in a sunny snow,
And half in azure air,
The cloudlet, pausing, loth to go
And leave the mountain bare,
With hazy hair
And misty feet in a sunny snow,
May not linger there;
Lithely curled in a merry breeze,
With look still turned to earth,
Wafted on viewless presences
From the mystic mount of birth,

With a merry mirth,
Summoning fondly as he flees,
" O father, leave your earth! "
Floating fair into sunny sky,
Evanishing away,
Praying the pine-veiled heights to fly;
Dark furrowed heights of grey;
" Away! away! "
" Our roots are deep, we may not die,"
Stern crags responded wearily;
" Fly thou away,
O child of day!
The hallowing of thy sunny smile,
Thy fingers of cool mist,
Soothed my weary soul erewhile,
And since thy lips have kissed,
Lightning, blast, nor lashing rain,
Snows nor howling hurricane
Mar my deep rest,
Remembering thy heavenly smile;
Fade thou away!
And leave me grey!"

EARLY PRIMROSE

THERE was a paly primrose,
Budding very early
In the little garden,
When he lay so ill.
" Do you think I may be
Well enough to go there
When the flower opens,
Papa?" he asked of me.
But only a day after
Our little Sunshine left us,
And the primrose opened
The very day he died.
I wonder if he saw it,
Saw the flower open,
Went to pay the visit
Yonder after all!
I know we laid the flower
On a stilly bosom

Of an ivory image;
But I want to know
If indeed he wandered
In the little garden,
Or noted on the bosom
Of his fading form
The paly primrose open;
How I want to know!

SLEEP

AIRILY the leaves are playing
In blue summer light,
Fugitive soft, shadow laying
Lovingly o'er marble white
Where he lies asleep.

Lilies of the valley bending
Lowly bells amid the green;
Sweet moss roses meekly lending
Their soft beauty to the scene
Of his quiet sleep.

All around him heather glowing
Purple in the sun;
Sound of bees and bird o'erflowing
Lull my lost, my little one,
Lying there asleep.

Harsher sight or sound be banished,
For my child is gone to rest;
These are telling of my vanished
In the language of the blest,
Wake him not from sleep!

IN THE CORSICAN HIGHLANDS

CLOUD-CHAOS surges o'er a crest sublime,
That seems forked lightning spellbound
    into stone;
Abruptly steep flame-pointed precipices,
Dark as the night, dissolve to opaline
In phantom foldings of circumfluent sea.
Their natures blend confused; the mists
    assume
A semblance of impenetrable rock;
Stern rock relents to luminous faint cloud.

Their banners rent as in uproarious war,
Behold! the vaporous battalions
Unclose, dispelled and routed of loud winds,
That drive them scared and scattered; so
    Jehovah
Clove that astounded sea for Israel.
Yonder beneath me, the enormous crag

Reveals, between grey ghostly robes of them,
Solid and rude and perpendicular,
A mighty front of Titans grandly piled,
Umber and gory red and pallid green,
Reared in some alien world beyond the cloud,
Stronghold stupendous of immortal gods.

The rude, immense, straight pillars of grey
    pine
Scale heaven, sustaining tempest writhen
    roofs
Of scant, green, level umbrage; they are
    built
Athwart yon vaporous and vastly walls
Of far off mountain; over them arise
Ruinous tower, fantastic pinnacle,
And icy spire in a blue burning air.
They over-hang deep forest-filled ravines
Wandering sea-ward; whose dim serpentine
Night ever hears a solemn utterance
Of torrents, with deep monotone attuned
To these wind-oracles of ancient pine.
Yonder a gaunt trunk-Skeleton upbraids
With blasted arms the Bolt that shattered it.
Tusky black monsters reign within the gloom
Of forest and dead waters desolate:

Dim mists drive blindly through portentous
    trees,
While a weird Sun blinks dwarfed within
    the drift:
Legions of shadowy shaggy ilex climb
Yon narrow-cloven hollows of the crag.

Now evening falls: an aromatic breath
Of amber oozing from a dun red bark,
And mountain herb and many a mountain
    flower
Pervades the air slow clearing from the
    cloud:
A vase-like cleft between two snowy peaks
Glowingly fills with a pale violet:
Beneath appears fair Ocean's purple line,
Far away from far portals of the pass.
Lower, a surge of huge dun purple rock
Tumultuously contorted, rolls a rude
And shadowy chaos interposed between
Dark peaks and me: Night's ever-deepening
    gloom
Engulfs the gorges: All is mighty Music,
Phantasmal symphony of ghostly Form,
A visionary Chorus with no sound.

Stern-visaged Isle! upon thy rocky breast
Two sons were nurtured, heritors of fame.
The one drew pride and ruin from thy veins,
Towering portentous, terrible, alone,
A scourge of God: Napoleon drew power
To desolate the world; while Paoli
Drank from dark fountains of thy resolute
    blood
The patriot's unshamed integrity.

Behold I stand within a place of graves:
Low wooden crosses o'er the lonely dead.
Within the wondrous amphitheatre
Of mountains overshadowing they rest;
Watched, warded in those awful arms they lie.
Ah! Nature here hath roused herself to robe
Her oft unheeded royalty in robes
Of godlike splendour, that our eyes may see;
Hath sounded as with trumpet blast of doom
That our dull ears may slumber not but
    hear!
Brands with fierce fire upon the heedless
    heart
Her names of wonder! yea, I know ye now:
I bow my head in worship: yea I feel
Your majesty of godlike Presences;

Stand here abashed with mortal head bowed
    low
Before you, Angels, Demons of the Lord!

Yet with no rapture of strong youth's acclaim
I hail you as a lowlier brother may
Hail a liege lord, a hero or a king,
But I have come into your awful courts,
A poor blind broken pilgrim from afar,
Who faltering chances upon some august
Assembly of dread princes, and bows low,
Yet only craves to learn if haply he,
Who used to lead his poor blind footsteps on
With such clear-seeing love, a little child
Who has been lost to him, alas! for long,
And whom he vainly seeks about the world,
About the dreary, barren world, be here?
But meeting no response to his demand
He can but idly weep a moment ere
He grope his weary way abroad again.

These are but void and ruined courts to me
Of faded splendour, unremembered Power!
I cannot see aright, I cannot feel.
And while men prate of knowing all the laws,
The mortal cold possessing human hearts

Weighs down their eyes in deep sepulchral
   gloom.
But if some Angel's sword from forth the night
With vasty voice of Doom, by human tongues
Called thunder, leapt, and smote me out of all
These evil dreams named living, might I find
My little child, and with him find the Lord?

We journey ever higher, through a grove
Of moon-lit chestnut, where a babbling stream,
At intervals, in open forest glades,
Flashes with ruffled, wandering, pale flame.
The air is richly laden with sweet spoil
From fragrant flower and foliage faint-green;
Shadowy-folded hills and dells involved
Whisper of verdure lush, luxuriant,
Known to fair elves, or rills who tinkling glide
Telling sweet secrets, haunted of shy beams,
Whene'er the whims of leafy Ariels
And cloudy gossamer aloft allow
Their gentle wandering; tall asphodel
And flowery fennel, either side our way
Often we dim discern; but where the woods
No longer in their colonnades of gloom
Involve our path, beyond the precipice,
Behold! how all the regions of the north,

Height, depth and breadth are held, filled,
   dominated
By one supreme pale presence, Monte d'Oro!
His spirit robes far floating, a dim grey,
Sombre with forest, pallid with the moon,
His kingly crest snow-gleaming to the stars.

Pan is not dead! He lives! He lives for ever!
These awful demiurgic Powers named Nature
Nourish, involve, a half-alive blind soul,
A human soul who fondly deems them dead.
Surely the Lord is making us alive!
Mine aching wound shall heal; for I shall find
My lost for whom I long; from thee my friend,
The weary burden of thy doubt shall pass.
Sorrow and wrong are pangs of a new birth:
All we who suffer bleed for one another;
No life may live alone, but all in all;
We lie within the tomb of our dead selves,
Waiting till One command us to arise.

ONLY A LITTLE CHILD

A Voice.

ONLY a little child!
  Stone cold upon a bed!
s it for him you wail so wild,
As though the very world were dead?
        Arise, arise!
    Threaten not the tranquil skies!

Do not all things die?
  'Tis but a faded flower!
Dear lives exhale perpetually
  With every fleeting hour,
Rachel for ever weeps her little ones;
For ever Rizpah mourneth her slain sons.
        Arise, Arise!
    Threaten not the tranquil skies!

Only a little child!
  Long generations pass:
Behold them flash a moment wild
  With stormlight, a pale headlong mass
Of foam, into unfathomable gloom;
Worlds and dead leaves have all one doom.
        Arise, arise!
  Threaten not the tranquil skies.

Should Earth's tremendous Shade
  Spare only you and yours?
Who regardeth empires fade
  Untroubled, who impassive pours
Human joy, a mere spilt water,
Revels red with human slaughter!
        Arise, arise!
  Threaten not the tranquil skies,

Another Voice.

  . . . Only a little child!
  He was the world to me.
Pierced to the heart, insane, defiled,
  All holiest hope! foul mockery,
Childhood's innocent mirth and rest;
Man's brief life a brutal jest.
        There is no God;
  Earth is Love's sepulchral sod!

Another Voice.

Only a little child
  Ah! then, who brought him here?
Who made him loving fair and mild
  And to your soul so dear?
His lowly spirit seemed divine,
Burning in a heavenly shrine.
              Arise, arise!
  With pardon for the tranquil skies.

Only a little child!
  Who sleeps upon God's heart!
Jesus blessed our undefiled,
  Whom no power avails to part
From the life of Him Who died
And liveth, whatsoe'er betide!
              Whose are eyes
  Tranquiller than starlit skies!

Only a little child!
  For whom all things are:
Spring and summer, winter wild,
  Sea and earth, and every star,
Time, the void, pleasure and pain,
  Hell and Heaven, loss and gain!
Life and death are his, and he

Rests in God's eternity.
Arise, arise!
Love is holy, true, and wise,
Mirrored in the tranquil skies.

GOD'S CHILD

HE wanders round the garden wild,
  I hear him singing sweet;
I know it is my fairy child,
  I hear his dancing feet.

Birds low warble in the nest,
  Leaves murmur merrily;
My boy is leaning on the breast
  Of God most tranquilly.

He gazes in deep eyes Divine
  With innocent clear eyes;
He is God's baby more than mine;
  The Father is all-wise.

Carol, my darling! laugh and leap!
  For art thou not God's own?
. . . Ah! wildly, wildly must I weep . . .
. . . God hath destroyed His son!

Stabbed with a sudden traitor thrust
  The heart so unafraid!
Then flung him down into the dust,
  To perish on the blade!

Earth felt, and, staggered with the blow,
  Reeled shuddering under me!
Dead worlds, like shrivelled leaves, fell low
  From Life's uprooted tree!

How shall I name Thee, Thou Supreme?
  Hate, Treachery or Crime?
. . . When may we rise from our dark dream
  Beyond the bounds of Time.

He is but folded closer still
  Within the Father's bosom,
Lest our earth airs may work him ill,
  My baby boy, my blossom!

MUSIC AND THE CHILD

I

An organ player comes rarely round
To our lone moorland place;
My darling at the welcome sound
Runs with laughter in his face
To the nursery window, hailing,
With melodious mirth unfailing,
The sun-burnt, black-bearded man,
Who greets him in Italian.
Then he brings and sets a chair,
Humming over every air,
Feigns to turn a handle deftly,
Feigns to talk Italian swiftly,
Fair in little blouse of blue,
Sweet of heart and form and hue.

Pale my love, with dews of anguish
From the night beneath his curls,
Lies asleep; and while we languish
In despair, behold! there purls
A rill of music from afar:
Can the favourite organ jar
So upon our hearts? we fear
Lest it waken him; yet hear
Him, waking, pray for it to come
Under the window of his room,
Asking that his friend, the player,
May have food; we grant the prayer.
Then he lists to every tune,
Growing very weary soon.

III

Baby lies upon the bed,
And our hearts with him lie dead.
Baby lies with fair white blossom
In his hair and hand and bosom:
  Only he is lovelier far
Than earth's fairest flowers are!
And while we cower, smitten low
By our baby boy's death-blow,
Draws again the organ near...
Ah! Baby never more may hear.

IV

When the little child was going,
From his lips came softly flowing,
Flowing dreamily the tune
Of a hymn that asks a boon
In childish accents of the Saviour
Who, by the love in his behaviour
Showed God cherishes a child;
And whensoe'er pain made him wild,
His mother sang it; then released,
The child himself sang on, nor ceased
On earth till he commenced in Heaven.
For I think that fatal even,
While upon death's wave he drifted
While the mist of life was lifted,
On our earth-shore he heard his mother,
And pure angels on the other;
We and they hearing the low voice of him
    who travelled
Between us, darkling, a wee pilgrim who
    the mystery unravelled!

Even so she sang to him,
While his lovely eyes grew dim
In fair former eves, while he
Loosed waifs of singing dreamily,
Till he floated into sleep.
Now it is more strange and deep.
"Jesu" he murmured, hearing the Lord call:
" Fear not, My darling, on My heart to fall!"

V

Then in the depth of our despair,
A vision found me lying there.
She and I were cowering
Before the swoop of Death's dark wing,
That sweeping him to nothingness,
Plunged our souls in the abyss,
Stone-eyed to stare upon the gloom,
Frantic to challenge the deaf tomb,
Beating upon its iron door
For him who shall return no more!
Death echoing from his awful vault
In ghastly mockery of our assault!
Wanderers ever, wanting only one,
Calling upon the name of our lost little son!

But I dreamt that she and I
Were gazing very mournfully
On the organ, as we deemed
Disused and broken. Then it seemed
That his dear nurse, who loved him well,

And cherished more than I can tell,
Came unaware, and on her breast
She bore him whom we laid to rest,
Our darling, glorious, health-rosed,
Whose dark dewy eyes reposed
On some far-off, enrapturing vision
Of the children's realm elysian!
Ah! with what transport we kissed him!
Not dead! not dead! howe'er we missed him!
Heaven too vouchsafes another token;
The little organ was not broken!
Lo! baby turns it round and round,
Rejoicing in the wonted sound,
Yea, singing in his blouse of blue,
Lovelier than we ever knew.

VI

While he lay nightly racked with pain,
Wept and shrieked the hurricane.
Yea, on that terrible night he died,
The clamour of fell fiends, beside
Themselves with hell's blaspheming anger,
Exultant in his god-wept languor,
Seemed to hound him on to death,
Hungry for his innocent breath!
But now what raves it for, and howls
Around with moan of drifted souls!
Are ye not satiate with such
A pure white victim to your clutch
Yielded by the Powers above,
Who yet we dare to dream are Love?
The loveliest, most heavenly-hearted
Child ever by themselves imparted
To this poor earth of ours!
                          So moaning
In fierce despair amid the groaning
Of those evil blasts I heard

A still small voice as of a bird.
Nay, bird had ne'er so sweet a voice,
Nor ever bird may so rejoice;
No spring that babbles in the summer
Nor flower-enamoured fairy hummer!
What is it, Lord? can it be human
Song of child or song of woman?
Some loving Ariel doth toy
In self-abandonment of joy;
Like, yet unlike our vanished angel!
I know I deem it an evangel
From my darling hovering
In the very storm to sing
Near my yearning soul, to tell
What seems the blasphemy of hell
Is love, to him who loveth well!

. . . In bluest air the melody
On silver wings appears to fly;
And lo! in live germander blue
A threefold flower-cluster flew,
Child-seraphim, arrayed in white,
Fair with dewy eyes of light;
As when two swallows on the wing,
Circle each other dallying;
In playful love we hear them cleaving

Blue air with dances they are weaving ;
So on tender pulsing pinion
Audibly the heaven's dominion
Many a threefold flower-band
Of children clove, while in their bland
Spirit wreathing, when one passed,
Shadow delicate fell fast
From him upon a sister child,
Softening to mood more mild
Her raptured whiteness undefiled.

VII

When the jubilant hymnals roam,
Buoyant-winged as sunny foam,
High-flung, wind-wafted, in the dome
Or solemn branched cathedral aisle,
From pure boy-bosoms, all the while
To me it seems my darling mingles
With the sound that burns and tingles,
Floating calm in the calm sea
Of all unshadowed harmony.
Holy, Holy, Holy! mount
Arrowy song-flight from the fount
Of our earth music! that descending
Erst from Heaven will be blending
Now with his full songs of joy
Who, lark-like sings where no alloy
Of earth a gentle soul may trouble
In her perennial sweet bubble,
Whose lily petal ever fair
Reposes feeding in live air.

NATURE AND THE DEAD

("He is made one with nature."—*Shelley.*)

I

I MUSED below dark everlasting rocks,
Hearing the circling happy seamew cry;
I listened to the gentle water-shocks
Of cool clear emerald, how peacefully
Wandering through cavern, hall, or labyrinth
Worn in the Cliff's heart! flowering seathrift
Sang to blithe bees and breezes; the red plinth
Of ocean-palace pillar in a lift
And fall of playful sunny wavelets glowed;
Until I floated on the hyaline
Into a mystic ocean fay's abode,
Hung with pale sea-grape, walled with
   coralline,
Gemmed with live jade and garnet, or adorning
Of gleaming opal-hearted passion-flowers,
Living, blue, crimson as a radiant morning;

95

While wavelight all the rocky temple dowers,
Golden, blood-jasper, grey, with woven smiles
Quavering musical, 'mid velvet piles
Wine-dark, fern-tufted; I am afloat in froth,
That seethes and sparkles on a heaving clear
Sunned chrysoprase; hued like a burnet-moth
Here the cliff shows, shell crusted wholly here
With shells, bathing their lucid filaments
In lapsing crystal; among twilit grots,
Fulfilling strange mysterious intents,
I hear far waters commune in dim spots
With weird rock comrade, monsters, fish or
      seal
Or slumberous anemones that feel.
Through yon chaotic arch of vasty height,
Of grand proportion, hewn by Titan hand
Of turbulent tempest, flying in blue light
Appear white sails, and capes of basking land,
Rich hazy brown; here towering dread forms
Of silent crag brood awful and alone:
These have absorbed all terror of the storms,
That wear, combat, caress their writhen stone.

My soul then said to Earth and Air
"How can I deem that ye would dare
To smile and dally if ye did
The deed of darkness? holding hid
My stolen child, my withered blossom,
Plucked, trampled, dead in your dark bosom!
If at the heart of your mad glee
My living child lay lifelessly!
And all your horrible vampire life
With his precious blood were rife!
If your false innocence but rave
Over a murdered infant's grave!
And all his wondrous soul blown out,
Your idiot salt billows flout
My child's pale corpse within your cave!
And this the end of him who lent
Blue heaven to my dull firmament!
Of him whose holy opening flower
Claimed eternity for dower!
Who from our green lowly sod

With wee white hands reached up to God,
Yea, talked familiarly with Him
As with myself, ere earth grew dim
With his strange silence, and the loss
That stole from beauty all her gloss
And charm for ever! left the world
A faded mouldering banner furled,
Once thundering glorious, impearled,
Aflame with morning! Mockery!
Curse your fair bodies with no heart!
Ah me! Alas! When I depart,
Shattered upon your iron rocks,
Stifled in wild water shocks,
Shall I not find within the gloom,
There in the darkness of my doom,
A dewy dawn of one who left
Me moaning when my heart was cleft?
A sweet auroral rising of my sun,
Who went out unaware, before his course
      was run,
And I lay darkling ere my day was well
      begun?"

III

But in a tone remonstrant, mild,
Like one who soothes a fevered child,
Methought fair Earth and Sky and Sea
Responded very quietly:
" Do you, then, our poor brother, ask
If all we wear the traitor's mask
On this our festival of gladness?
We pity, pardoning, your madness!
He is not dead whom you so cherish!
How may a human spirit perish?
Spirits! ye dream a lovely dream,
And call it what we only seem!
Ye call us Nature: we are angels,
Who reveal profound evangels,
Though you may fathom not their glory
Beholding as in sacred story,
Men like trees walking: so God gives
Maturing sense to all that lives.
But once ye dwelt in Eden—then
We were gods who dwelt with men;

Your antenatal sphere remember;
Clear the earth-ash from the ember!
Spirits immortal! all we live and move
In One Whose name is the Eternal Love.
Yea, with flame-clasp of suffering
Christ's own divine embraces cling!
Your little one is only gone up higher,
Burns now, and glows with more seraphic
    fire:
For this we bound him to the funeral pyre!
Yea, folded closer, closer to our breast,
His accents reach you from our radiant rest,
Mingling with ours! Ah! with sweet sur-
    prise
Awake! and hear! believe! and recognize!"

    Sark.

THE TOY CROSS

My little boy at Christmas-tide
    Made me a toy cross;
Two sticks he did, in boyish pride,
    With brazen nail emboss.

Ah me! how soon, on either side
    His dying bed's true cross,
She and I were crucified,
    Bemoaning our life-loss!

But He Whose arms in death spread wide
    Upon the holy tree,
Were clasped about him when he died —
    Clasped for eternity!

AZRAEL

I was bending o'er my treasured infant,
O'er his infernal bed of pain;
All my spirit cloven to its foundations,
Echoing his cries again,
They went crashing through my brain.
Till there came a hollow, hollow knocking
At my darling's lowly chamber door,
And my tortured heart sank fainting in me,
For I knew who stood before.
Then I beheld a dumb and dreadful Presence,
Shrouded in long rigid folds of grey,
Never daring to unveil its awful visage
Before the blessed day.
I, confronting barred the lowly entrance;
Yea, I flung my bleeding soul athwart.
I swore, "Thy touch shall ne'er pollute my
    holy one
Till thou tread upon my heart!

Swift-souled he is and pure and fair and happy,
All his life yet pausing in the bud;
He is mine eyes, the pulse of all my being,
Vital warmth and dancing blood!
I have looked along the flowery vistas
Of his lovely paradisal spring;
I have mused and seen myself beholding
His innocence upon the wing,
Flying in the freshly lilied alleys,
Blithely singing ever a sweet rhyme.
Wilt thou strike him dead before me? wilt
   thou leave me
In blind silence for all time?
I shall look for long upon his opening beauty,
See the sail fill of his gallant youth,
Fair unsheathing of a generous keen spirit
Flashing eager for the Truth!
He shall defend us and delight us, old and
   weary,
His poor weeping mother there and me!
Will it melt thee pondering how long and
   dreary
Without him all our way will be?
How we longed and prayed and waited
   for him!
And when, fairer than fond Hope could claim

He arrived among us, how our hearts leaped
Blessing, loving as he came!"

Falling prone, I grovelling entreated,
"Dreadful Deity! for once be kind!"
But, implacable, It icily swept o'er me
A mighty moaning wind;
And I saw my baby in its drear embraces,
Rigid, cold and silent, smitten dead.
Yet while I lay and impotently cursed It,
Methought, before It fled,
In place of Azrael, the awful angel,
When a fold fell from the countenance,
Methought I saw, O miracle; the Saviour,
With a world's love in His glance!
I beheld divinely human eyes of Jesus.
Unfathomable seas of sorrowing;
I saw like flame upon the riven forehead
His martyr-crown of King!
"Pardon, Lord!" I cried, "O take my
    darling!"
Looking in His Face methought He smiled.
Ere they vanished, in the empty chamber
    kneeling,
I yielded him my child.

And I felt a little babe may on a stranger
For a while a fondling joy confer,
Yet if he hear the low tone of his mother,
He will bound away to her.
Were we high and pure enough to be the
    guardians
Of a heavenly soul so pure and high?
God, Who lent our bird out of His bosom
Recalls him to the sky!
If He brought him to us, He can keep him
Safer than our foolish feeble care;
It is very blind of us to weep him
Removed from our sad air,
Moved to where the holy ones are telling
In pure white lilies the Lord's love
Where amaranth and asphodel a dwelling
Weave around our dove,
Full of wisdom, full of love!

Was it very, very lonely, O my darling!
Very lonely for a little child,
Whom we cherished so, and guarded in his
    goings,
Carried from us to the wild,
When thy dear bewildered eyes looked back
    upon us,

And we longed in vain to keep thee or to
   follow,
Longed for glimpses of thee disappearing
In the gloomy, guilty hollow?
Ah! if we had seen thee, with companions
Coming forth to meet thee with a smile,
For there are to whom the beatific vision
Hath been granted otherwhile,
While they weeping stood deserted on the
   desert,
And love was borne o'er wan waves far
   away!
Yet the Lord of life and death is ever near us,
If we go or if we stay.
Lo! the same mild moon upon the wanderer
Looks, and on the dweller by the hearth;
So the mild large Eye of the All-Father
Wards all worlds and earth,
Raining a sweet influence of spirits,
For no malignant ray can harm the pure:
It was Jesus, and the gentle saints departed
Who came his wound to cure;
On their gentle bosom how secure!

If I only knew how I shall behold him,
When and where and in what happy guise!

Will he be a child when I enfold him?
Or will the form change as he grows more
    wise
He will ever be a child in his sweet spirit!
And I deem the very form will never die;
But Ah! the soul slides where she holds
    no image!
Reels nor grasps reality!
If I were only sure of his well being,
Sure as I am of anguish here,
Could I wish him in our foul, infected prison,
Away from his pure air.

Ah! Thy merciless stern mercy hath chas-
    tised us,
Goading us along the narrow road;
Thy bird who warmed and dazzled us a
    moment,
Hath returned to Thine abode,
Lord when we are purged within the furnace,
May we have our little child again?
All Thine anguish by the olives in the Garden,
All Thy life and death are vain,
If Thou yield us not our own again!

A SOUTHERN SPRING CAROL

O SPRING! O Spring! O Southern Spring!
What a triumphal song you sing!
All the valley sings!
Nor only warblers who have wings;
All the peach and almond blossom
Seems young carol from their bosom
In the form of flowers,
Wandering every way
On many a spray,
Rills in the blue day,
Very bird-notes in a spray
Filling all the valley.
And I deem that, as they dally
In the summer light intense,
In the deep Italian blue,
A subtle spirit influence
May re-enchant them to a dew
Of melody pure-hearted,

Hither and thither parted
From the bosom of the birds,
From the gaily feathered herds,
And they would be songs again,
One rich rain!
A peach petal flutters down,
A white moth hath softly flown,
And we hardly know sweet note
From fair vision as they float.
All the valley sings!
An angel kindles when he dips
The fig's candelabra tips
To chrysolite, while many a vine
Amorously will incline
O'er vistas of a golden trellis
Where a cool and shadowy well is,
All overgrown with mosses wet
And maiden-hair and violet.
O'er many a shrine
Roses twine!
Light green fountains of the palm
Fall in a blue crystal calm;
Delicate flushing lady tulips
Close their lanceolate dim dew-lips,
Their soft satiny repose
By a light hand flecked with rose;

Golden jonquils, white narcissus,
Whisper softly, "Come and kiss us!
Part us not from the sweet brood
Of our companions in the wood!"
Earth's fair features, every one
Instinct with spirit of the sun,
Radiate well-married hues,
Blent with air and ocean blues.
Verily I seem to stand
In a realm of fairyland,
Or I take my dazzled station
In some intense illumination
Of a missal mediæval
Yonder on the hill's upheaval
Where we hear the convent chime,
Wrought by monk of olden time,
Whom the cloister heard intone,
And many a sun-bleached river stone,
Or the darkling cypress cone.
Cool grey clouds of olive fill
All the foldings of the hill,
While fair dawn-empetalled peaches
Gleam athwart the bloomy reaches
Of quiet hare-bell mantled mountain
Gemmed with rivulet or fountain,
Shadowy evening robes whose hem

Shines with many a water gem:
While rich oranges all golden,
In a darkling foliage holden,
Are a foil to the pale gleaming
Of oval lemon, and the beaming
Ampler cherry trees, one snow
Of blossom in the fading glow!
In pale blue evening,
Ah! the cherry seems to sing,
With a fairy bridal dower!
Pure white chalices of flower,
Pendent in a pale blue sky,
Shadowy blossom with soft eye!
Dimlit amber mysteries
We faint surmise
Where bees hover
And a soft moth lover!
Oh, I would that I might know
The secret of your bridal snow,
Soul of the pure ecstasy
Softly haunting a grey sky,
With such a grace
Of spirit-lace!
For it seems a happy ghost
From the seraph host!
Never bride dissolved in love,

Never saint in realms above,
Nor lark on his own music tost
Hath more joy than this, embossed,
Shadowy, rare,
On pale blue air;
White cloud a-flower,
A very shower
Of still rapture unalloyed,
Too overjoyed
For sound of singing!
All the valley sings!
A clear rivulet is flinging
Warbled song to the pure air,
Laughing, a young infant fair,
Ruffling softly, swiftly passes
Green-illumined among grasses,
Or red anemone to wander,
Where are violet, germander;
Child pursued in play, to ramble,
After such a sweet preamble
Among myrtle bowers and bramble.
Green-pennoned cane-brakes in the river
All around grey arches quiver;
While westering Apollo dulls
Delved loam and vivid pulse,
A swart red-vestured toiler waters

From rills, who are the river's daughters.
All the valley sings!
And rings, and rings!
Ah! Nature never would have power
To breathe such ecstasy of flower,
Vernal songs of happy birds,
The young rill's delicious words,
No iris hues might bring to birth,
No heart were hers for any mirth,
If he were turned to common earth!
If a child so fair, so good,
Were a waif on Lethe's flood,
If a soul-source of feeling, seeing,
Were blotted from the realms of being!
She from all delight would start.
With such a horror at her heart,
She would reel dissolved, and faint
With deep dishonour of the taint!
The very girders of her hall
Crushed, her stately floor would fall.
Ourselves are the foundation stone;
If thought fail, the world is gone;
All were ruined, wanting one.
But all the valley sings!
Nature rises on immortal wings!
And soaring, lo! she sings! she sings!

There is no death!
She saith.
O Spring! O Spring! O Southern Spring!
What a triumphal song you sing!

Valley of Taggia, 1880.

ALL SAINTS, AND ALL SOULS

THY birthday is All Saints' Day, my sweet
    treasure.
    Ah! well it may be!
For on us there descended in full measure
All saints in one celestial pleasure,
With thee, dear baby!
For thou wert open, loyal, fearless,
    Ah me! forsaken!
Radiant soul in raiment peerless,
A private joy to thee how cheerless,
    Until partaken!
It is All Saints' Day; on the morrow,
    With flowers offered,
Sons and daughters of dark sorrow
Some faint ray of peace may borrow
    From flowers proffered
On green mounds of the departed.
    Meekly saying

To sweet souls of the true-hearted,
"May we not for long be parted,
   Here delaying!"
There a friend, a sister, mother,
   Fondly kneeling,
Sobs and tears are fain to smother,
Unto the dear sundered other
   Self appealing,
"Leave me not alone, O lover!
   Child I cherish!"
"May the reign of love be over?
Death is only sent to prove her!
   May she perish?"
In warm-breathing blue ethereal
   White tapers kindled
Shyly waver, souls aerial,
In all-beholding strength imperial
   Of Day dwindled,
Like our lives in the universal
   Sun of spirit;
Hark how ocean makes rehearsal
Of a life without reversal
   All inherit!
An eternal child, blue Ocean,
   Rhythmic breathing
O'er the dead, with grand emotion,

And blue hills with deep devotion
    Hearts are wreathing.
We are sure they are not sleeping
    Beneath our blossom,
By white marble we may, weeping,
Plant for memory, but keeping
    Near our bosom
Life's own vigil o'er us, even
    As in dreaming
O'er what seems their sleep, bereaven,
We hold our vigil; they in heaven
    Know no seeming!

San Remo.

VISION OF THE NIGHT

A SOFT young moon among the trees
Nor lights the valley-side, nor these
Only faint illumes a hill
Far over me, where pale and still
A fane mid habitations fair,
Gemmed with mild fires, inhabits air
Of clear May midnight; nightingales
Lull the lonely-lying vales;
Living stars above are set,
As in adoration met.
Yon hill appears a holy hope,
Far beyond our earthly scope,
Ghostly gleaming in the cope
Of heaven, revealed, anon withdrawn.
But I have felt the vision dawn,
Hallowing my lowly lawn.
So I may wait, tho' all be gloom,
Till the eternal day illume.
    Ceriana.

IN LONDON

THE mighty towers of Westminster
Loom beneath me in murk air,
While a vast expanse of street
Echoes to loud hurrying feet
Of men and horses and swift wheels,
Where a clanging steeple peals,
Where he who with deep feeling cons
The souls of animals, in bronze
Wrought majestic lion forms,
Brooding, slumbering, dark storms,
Symbols of our England's power,
Whose dread lightnings brood and glower,
Like those fulvous eyes; their claws
Are death, hid sheathed in vasty paws.
On the lion a child gazes;
Grave brown wondering eyes he raises
To the form: compelled to leave,
With all my sight to him I cleave

In departing; often since
As from a sickening stroke I wince,
Journeying by the very place
Where I beheld his little face
Pondering on the mighty beast,
More than all to me, though least,
Seeing now through tear suffusion
Without him all the loud confusion!

Once again the living creatures,
With their weary sullen features,
I behold behind the bars
Where the den's dull limit mars
All wild splendour of their pride,
Abates the grandeur of their stride.
Bondage tames the fervid eyes,
As night doth the torrid skies,
To a lurid sultriness,
Clouded o'er with vague distress;
Emblems of our human race
Fallen from their lofty place,
Blind, bewildered, bound within
By the manacles of sin!

With a glad and grave surprise
The terror of their gleaming eyes

He considers, mirthful mime
Of them in a little time.
Again I view the elephant,
Slow-pacing in his wonted haunt,
On whose tall, broad, howdah'd back
The child and I along the track
Three years ago swung, full of glee—
Now the child is not with me!

When our wild praying seemed to stir
God's awful executioner,
Whose blank, set countenance faint quavered
Whose dull resolve a moment wavered,
And when sweet life seemed to repel
Death's white horror, it befell
That when he would descend the stair,
Patient he paused for one to bear
Him feeble, and I filled the want;
So he named me his elephant.

Passing through the gay ancade
Where toys for children are displayed,
Anon I pause before a toy,
Dreaming how a little boy
Will lighten mirth from his dear face
If I buy it—for a space

Unremembering my home
Without him is but blind and dumb!
His sacred toys lie idle now;
O'er them the pale anguished brow
Of Love's forlorn despair we bend,
Hoping life's dull pain may end;
Till anon some organ sounds
In the street, but no glad bounds
Of a child's light feet we note
Run to hear the music float,
Climb upon a chair to see
Dancing dolls, bedizened glee,
Or the monkey's mimicry.

What shall I do? . . . Full many others,
Little ones who seem his brothers,
Take delight in things like these!
Do they ail, or doth, the breeze
Of pleasure ripple o'er their faces,
I will contemplate their graces;
I will be a minister
The fountain of their joy to stir
In such resorts, and by such measures
As were wont to yield him pleasures;
Or where little hearts may ail,
Love's a yoke-fellow, I will not fail,

Where are tears and visage pale,
To quell the tyranny of Fate
Or man that renders desolate:
And I deem he will approve
In the bowers of holy Love,
Near and nearer to me move.
Ours, how weak soe'er be strife,
On the holy side of life!
How loud soe'er the world may roar,
We know Love will be conqueror!

DEATH

DEATH is very beautiful,
Solemn, pure and calm,
As in a shadowy cloister cool,
A lowly murmured psalm,
After some fierce battle cry
In the windy glare hard by.
Nay, very terrible is death!
A cold white shape of fear;
By it we talk with bated breath,
As if the thing could hear.
So like, and so unlike the face!
Ah! why borrow their dear grace?
Nay! thou cold mockery of life!
Death take any other guise!
If they with living joy be rife,
Why looks their image on this wise?
Why make us deem they turn to *this*
Who were the pulse of all our bliss?

Death is Satan's cruel jest,
His blaspheming parody!
" Lo! I give your darling rest;
Come and see him by-and-by!
Kiss the unanswering icy stone,
And know thyself alone, alone!
My repose is long and deep
Not a passing earthly sleep. "

Nay! this hath some inner sense;
I would resolve the mystery
'Tis but a symbol of intense
Unwearying life for these who die.
Lord! may we wake to see Thy face
And our beloved in Thine embrace?
We dream a dream of cold white death,
And all our being shuddereth.
Ah! when may we interpret, Lord,
The meaning of Thy mystic Word?

Death is very pitiful,
Death for a dear child!
A pure white bud some wanton pull
Scatters on the wild!
And yet woe may deeper move,
The dying and the death of Love!

He seemed so amiable, so fair,
All holy, a perennial youth!
Dumb and stark he lieth there;
God Himself may weep for ruth.
"Dear Love, perchance may not be dead,
Only sleeping", some one said.
Ah! death is very beautiful
Solemn, pure, and calm,
As in a shadowy cloister cool,
A holy chanted psalm,
After some fierce battle cry
In the windy glare hard by,
Singing, "We are saved from evil,
From the wandering waves' upheaval,
Folded far from very death,
Wherein the spirit withereth. "

GUARDIAN ANGELS OF CHILDREN

VERILY their angels
Ever behold the face
Of our eternal Father
Sunned in His full grace.
Yet in the stormless sunshine
They do not love to dwell;
There is no place in Heaven
They love half so well
As the lowly chamber
Of a little child,
Dearer to them the breathing
Of his bosom mild
Than are all the pæans
Round about the throne,
Scorning the cold splendour
Of an idle crown.
Love rears her radiant palace

In our shadow-world of fears,
She mourns by our dark ocean
Of tempestuous tears!
Angels tend the children
Waking or asleep,
They rebuke the evil
Who have made them weep.
Heaven's crystal glory gloweth
Rainbowed as they fly
To where earth's night illumined
In their sweet charity,
Dawneth silently!

In the lordly castle
In the dungeon deep,
In the lonely hovel,
Love-vigil they keep.
Fair be the children, cherished,
Sweethearted, rosed with health,
Or poor and starved and wanting
The soul's holier wealth,
Inheritors of sorrow,
By leaguering ills deformed,
Plague-smitten soul and body,
Poor hearts love never warmed,
With all the angels tarry;

And though the fire be low,
They will fan the ember
To a living glow;
Inhabiting our sorrow,
Our chilled heart of wrong,
Until it yield and mellow
Bloom to a sweet song.
They, knowing our mortal fever
Soon will pass away,
Through long nights of sorrow
Calm await the Day.
Asleep they lead the lambkins
To meadows of sweet dream
In gentle arms they bear them
By many a cooling stream;
Where the sunbeams cherish
White and yellow flowers,
They may sail on silver
Among fairy bowers,
Losing all the terror
Of our waking world,
Sails of their frail shallop
In flowery havens furled.

A poor boy rides the pony
So wistfully admired,

While a poor maiden nurses
The doll richly attired;
They feel no more so tired!
Pains and griefs no longer
Vex the innocent breast,
Now dear angels lull them
Into such deep rest.
Cruel faces vanish
And all the loveless waste,
In a fair home they find them
Tenderly embraced.

And when we deem them dying,
More life the Lord imparts,
Their faint, frail breath subsideth
On warm angel hearts;
Like a wavelet failing
On a sand so fair:
Ah! then the angels welcome
Heaven's cloudless crystal air!
Because of the frail snow-flake
Their kind bosoms wear.
The snowflake melts in glory,
The little child awakes;
Under the smiles of Jesus,
Death-frozen for our sakes

There are no more snow-flakes!
With our snows bejewelled
How the angels shine,
Earth's frozen flower a sunlet
Pulsing light divine!

Dear babes, help one another!
All the saints help you:
We are with them in heaven,
Doing as they do.
Every cross of sorrow
Is a blessed pain;
The Lord Jesus bore it,
Proving it pure gain.

LAST VICTIMS FROM THE WRECK OF THE "PRINCESS ALICE"

I

Two little bodies, from the tide
Last gathered, lie alone;
No father maddens by the side
Of Love turned into stone
No mother weeps here for her pride,
Her joy for ever flown.
They were all innocence and mirth,
Warm light of loving eyes;
They are defiled and ruined earth,
The passing stranger flies.
The twain who watched them warmly curled,
Asleep with locks of gold,
Felt that for them the whole wide world
Nestled there aureoled.
And now they lie unknown, unnamed,

In London's awful roar;
Over them piteous, unclaimed,
Oblivion's dust will pour,
Love's eyes look never more!
There is no silver sound, no speech,
Although they rest so nigh
No rosy dimpled hands impleach
In slumber tranquilly.
From the close clasp of loving arms,
From heedless holiday,
Hurled upon death's dire alarms,
And to uncared for clay!

II

Are they indeed unknown, unnamed?
Is any life spilt water?
In the lone universe unclaimed!
Souls for mad chance to slaughter!
Have they no mother and no father?
In all the worlds no friend?
Are they a dim grey dust?—or rather,
Did our Eternal Parent send
Fair shining cohorts of His grace,
Strong children of His Love
Who minister before His face,
Swift thronging from above,
To gather them from forth the gloom,
Long ere men found their forms?
To shield them in the shock of doom,
While heavenliest ardour warms
With emulation every breast!
All will be first to hold,
To lull the frightened babes to rest
In their maternal fold!

There leaned both sire and mother lost,
Dawning on the dim gaze;
And many sealed in death's deep frost,
Fathers of former days,
Thronged all the approaches of God's throne,
While Christ arose above,
Smiling a welcome to His own
Babe brethren of His love.
. . . Yet ah! the hideous prospect whirls;
Death-slumber seems profound;
With ghastly gleams the river swirls
Blindly above the drowned!
. . . Nay, but the children are awake,
Although we hear them not;
Our dear ones their sweet prattle make
In some fair far cot.
I deem our life is a red flame
Of purgatorial fire;
And Death, God's calm white angel came
From the Eternal Sire,
To lay cool hands before their eyes,
Shadowing from the glare,
And in profound tranquillities
To hide from our despair.
    One pure white Light is over all,
One Spirit-Pulse serene,

Who when we rise and when we fall,
Unmoved approves the scene.
For Love is Lord from Heaven to Hell,
Walks our red waves of sorrow;
Love weeps beside us; all is well;
Day will dawn to-morrow.
Love weeps beside us, and within
Love moaneth for our lot;
Behold! his vassals Death and Sin,
Chained to His Chariot!
Love sleeps not, throned indifferent
Upon a lordly scorn;
He is the Man Whose brows are rent
With sorrow's crown of thorn.
God is the God-forsaken Man;
He is the Little Child;
His eyes with human woes are wan;
And all is reconciled!

CHILDREN AND THE WOODS

I LOVE the beautiful green woodland,
Where shy singing fairies flit;
In the twilight of their foodland
I hear a tapping while I sit,
And deem it is the woodpecker,
Yet know not other elfin noises
That waking near me softly stir,
While a shadowy bough faint poises,
Dreamily athwart the beryl
Of sensitive sun-lighted leaves;
And breathlessly as in play-peril,
The laughing rillet swiftly cleaves
A way through trees and flowers who love
    him,
Waving green arms while he flows,
With touch light hindering above him,
As they would kiss him while he goes,
But he merrily from them flows,

Blessing the green twilit heart,
As erst to mine my little one would songful
    light impart!

Ah! now my fairy brock is dry;
Where are the playful gleamings of his eye,
Or songs of his sweet innocent revelry?
But while I love the gentle woodland,
And fragrant pines that stir and sing
Hushfully in upland valleys,
Blue lakes and every living thing,
I love the little human children
Better than all woods and flowers,
The music of their innocent gambols
More than springs and summer showers.
And my heart is never lonely
If in roving I may meet
A few little children only
With their merrily flying feet,
In the play-field fresh from school,
Or among glades of woodland cool.
They are fair meanings of the daylight,
Clear fulfilment of meek flowers,
All a shyly wandering faylight
Would say among her leafy bowers.
In their sweet, shy, side-long glances,

And every lisping word that wells,
In their light aerial dances,
As of wind-waved lily-bells . . .
I think I hear his very tone,
I feel his very living smile;
Yea, one would says he lends his own
To these fair children for a while.
Dear Father, these are very fair;
Lovely in all their ways,
Whose every breathing is a prayer,
And all their motion praise.
Then a gleam steals o'er the snow
Of my low-responding breast.
Even as a faint after glow
Dawns in the ever-faded west.
And so God gives all babes to me,
In place of Baby who is gone;
Yet ah! the whole fair human family
Weighs lighter than my little one!

LEAD ME WHERE THE LILY BLOWS

FRIEND you tell me of a valley
  Where the pure white lily blows,
In a shadowy woodland alley
  Lead me to their summer snows!
      Oh, lead me where the lily blows!
      I would wear it in my life,
      Weary of world-soil and strife,
      Lead me where the lily blows.

Angels planted in my garden
  A vain pleasance of ill weeds,
One white lily, and the Warden
  With sweet air from heaven feeds.
Ah! one night my lily died,
  And I mourned him night and day;
"For the bosom of My Bride,"
  The Lord saith, "he was borne away."
Then I wandered through the world
  To find the flower de luce I lost,

And my wings will ne'er be furled,
  Summer-poised, or tempest-tost,
Till my lily of the valley
  Somewhen, somewhere, my spirit find,
In a sweet celestial alley,
  Far from our lost human-kind;
Ah! my lily of the valley!
     Lead me where the lily blows,
      I would wear it in my life,
      Weary of world-soil and strife
     Oh, lead me where the lily blows!

I wander till I find my flower
  Breathing a divine perfume;
His white petals are a power
  My lone spirit to illume:
And I will follow where the Lord
  Wills my weary feet to go,
While ever in my soul I hoard
  The glimpse allowed to me below
Of what belonged to Paradise
  Allowed awhile on earth to beam,
Until my weary wandering eyes,
  With patient use, more native seem
To shadowy regions of dim death;
  Till I faint behold my blossom,

No more in the outer Court have breath,
Earth's outer Court of life and death,
   As erst, but in my very bosom!
     In the Holiest of all
       By mine Altar in the gloom
       Behold my lily fair and tall,
       Breathing in immortal bloom!

Every lowly thing that feels,
   All we misname inanimate,
From one Eternal Heart appeals
   To every heart, as to a mate,
"Rejoice or weep, for our estate!"
So, if we love the Father's will,
Embrace the world and help mankind,
   Our lost lily-bell shall fill
With dewy morning soul and mind!
   For if mine be the true Lily
Whence all lily forms have birth,
   My holy child will blossom stilly
For me in his morning mirth,
     Fairer than he bloomed on earth!
       Lead me where the lily blows,
        I would wear it in my life,
         Weary of world-soil and strife,
        Oh, lead me where the lily blows!

"THAT THEY ALL MAY BE ONE"

WHENE'ER there comes a little child,
My darling comes with him;
Whene'er I hear a birdie wild
Who sings his merry whim,
Mine sings with him:
If a low strain of music sails
Among melodious hills and dales,
When a white lamb or kitten leaps,
Or star or vernal flower peeps,
When rainbow dews are pulsing joy,
Or sunny waves or leaflets toy,
Then he who sleeps
Softly wakes within my heart:
With a kiss from him I start;
He lays his head upon my breast,
Tho' I may not see my guest,
Dear bosom guest!
In all that's pure and fair and good,

I feel the spring-time of thy blood,
Hear thy whispered accents flow
To lighten woe,
Feel them blend,
Although I fail to comprehend.
And if one woundeth with harsh word,
Or deed, a child or beast or bird,
It seems to strike weak Innocence
Through him who hath for his defence
Thunder of the All-loving Sire,
And mine to whom He gave the fire.

CHRISTMAS EVE

SHIMMER of laughter
Glimmer of play
Flown in a wafture,
Blown in a spray,
From blithe floor and rafter
Over the way

I know it is feast-day, a
Mirth-day for all;
Oh, to the least may a
Birthday befall;
And the high priest play
There in the hall!
Play with his treasures;
He is a child,
Swaying their pleasures,
Being so mild;
The Holy One measures
Mirth for a child.

Weep we less wildly!
Sleeping is well;
The Lord hath laid on him
A wonderful spell.
Flower-band childly
Call away fear!
Our hand mildly
Tender you cheer!

How I muse of him
Gambolling so,
With all these who love him
A brief while ago,
Heaven's joy above him,
Our joy below!

Ah! may you be merry
While one is lost,
In his dear bosom the
Terrible frost?
Smile we who bury
All we love most?

Or is he hiding
Here in the hall,
And will he come gliding

Swift when we call?
Yea! I have found him,
Nor ever we part,
Love hath enwound him
Deep down in my heart!

"THE CLOUD MAY SAIL THERE"

THE cloud may sail there
Day flow and fail there,
And the eagle fly,
Haze overshadow
A smooth snow meadow,
And gleams of silver
Fleeting fly
From yon cloud delver
Of gleaming eye!
The moon may tarry with
Her pale bow,
And moonrise marry with
Virgin snow,
Blue heavens abide,
Or solemn-eyed
Stars by night, who gaze and go:
Ah! ne'er pollute
With a mortal foot

Yon realms of spirits aerial;
All but the lute
Of air be mute
From rosy morn to evening fall,
While flowerets blue
Fair with dew,
Laugh to the azure over all;
Let a music mazy
Born of the hazy
Play of a tender light and shade,
On hallowed ground
Dance with the sound
Fairy horns have faintly made;
A cloud of snow
Softly blow
Delicate verge of the form so white,
In a windy whirl;
But man, be far from the holy height
Soil no fair fields of frosty light!

"THE DESERT SHALL BLOSSOM AS THE ROSE"

THE desert way is dreary,
All empty is the wild,
My feet are very weary,
I cannot find my child.
The infinite blank spaces
Are weighing on my soul,
Gloom reigns in their dumb faces,
And there is no goal!
My hand is on the hollow
Where I dreamed a heart;
The world is dead; I follow,
Darling, where thou art!
But while my hope was swooning,
And Earth and Heaven reeled,
I heard an infant moaning,
Who to my love appealed:
So then I prayed for power,

And laid him on my breast;
The little human flower
Sank trustfully to rest—
But in the self-same hour
My form the cold earth pressed. . . .
. . . An orbed luminous haze-lily,
For pistil the Moon-pearl!
Ringed round with daffadowndilly,
A halo of brown curl,
As of young angels kneeling,
A reverent band aloof!
Earth smiles in the revealing
Of heaven's aery woof.
The stranger child I lifted
Wan lieth where he fell;
His scanty raiment rifted,
And woe-worn features tell
Of a life-long famine,
Of cruelty and pain:
And now while I examine
The piteous face again,
Meseems there dawns a kindred
To a long lost face;
While wakening unhindered
Wings of filmy grace
From the poor frayed swathings

Of his soiled garments break,
And delicate soft bathings
In the moon-sphere make.
Behold! they turn to flowers,
And settle in his hair
All over him in showers;
He hath grown so fair!
Christ in him overpowers
Dull strength of my despair:
While some sweet kindred gathers
To one fair face I love:
Ye divine it, fathers,
Who have a child above!
. . . Lo! an eyelid fluttered;
I know the bosom heaved!
. . . Now his own arms have uttered
All I disbelieved!
Dear eyes long held in durance,
For ever open wide,
To yield my soul assurance
Of all she hath denied!

FLOWER TO FLOWER

EUCHARIS lilies.
Roses red,
Lie on the form of the
Early dead;
Eucharis lilies
Roses white
Lie on the shrine of a
Jewel of Light!
Tho' the jewel be flown, o, the
Shrine is fair;
Flowers are breathing
Everywhere.
Within his bosom and
Wavy hair;
Flowers for emblem.
Flowers for faith,
Sweet mortal words
The Immortal saith!

Beautiful souls
Akin to his,
Who seem to be born
Out of all he is,
Who love to be born
And to die for this.
Flowers for rememberance
Flowers for truth;
Thoughts of the angel of
Innocent youth;
Dews of the morning
Over their mirth
Softly awaking
From sleep in earth;
Sweet resurrection,
A holy birth!
Red for renouncement,
Green is for hope,
White for humility,
Flowers who droop;
Pale for his purity
Fair they link,
Leaning a hand to us,
Ere we sink.
Azure for infinite
Heaven's embrace,

Tender and true
Celestial grace;
Red for the heart's blood
Of Christ our Lord;
Blue for His Love, who will
Keep His Word.
Pansy and violet,
Primrose pale,
Lily of the valley,
Folded frail,
And water-lily
Fulfil the tale.
Pansy and violet,
Lilies white,
All for the form of a
Lily of Light.

VALE!

O TENDER dove, sweet circling in the blue,
Whom now a delicate cloud receives from view
A cool, soft, delicate cloud, we name dim
    Death!
O pure white lamb-lily, inhaling breath
From spiritual ether among bowers
Of evergreen in the everliving flowers.
Yonder aloft upon the airy height,
Mine eyes may scarce arrive at thy still light!
Wandering ever higher, oh, farewell!
Wilt thou the dear God tell
We loved thee well,
While He would lend thee? Why may we
    not follow?
Do thou remember us in our dim hollow!
Farewell, love, oh! farewell, farewell, fare-
    well!
We wave to thee, as when of old

Thou waved and we waved, heart of gold!
Parting for a little while!
And is all parting only for a while?
O faint perfume from realms beyond the sky!
Waft of a low celestial melody!
O pure live water from our earthly well,
Whom Love changed to a heavenly œnomel
The while he kissed the bowl with longing lip,
And drew the soul therein to fellowship!
Shimmer of white wings ere ye vanish!
Glimmer of white robes, ere ye banish
With your full glory, mortal eyes
From Paradise!
So far, so far,
Little star!
Unless thine own dear happiness it mar,
Remember us in our low dell,
Who love thee well!
Farewell!

THE WATER-NYMPH AND THE BOY

I LIVE in the heart of a limpid pool,
In the living limpid heart of a pool:
I lie in a flow of crystalline,
Where silvery fish with jewelled eyne
Float silent and the ripple-gleam
With many a delicate water-dream
Moves the face of flowers to quaver,
Hanging where the wavelets waver;
Daffodil, hyacinth, spring flowers
Who slumber veiled from sunny showers,
That only trickle feebly through
Forest foliage from the blue.
My streamlet sparkles in the pines,
And here in lambent flame declines;
For the sun has burst his leafy thrall,
Kissing it passionate in the fall.
I love to feel the water plash

Merrily into my pool,
With a swift reverberating flash
Of soft foam beautiful.
One brilliant surface shrines the sky,
Another young lit leaves on high,
While yet another shadowed o'er
Below deep emerald, my floor
Reveals, all wavering below
My water's everlasting flow.
O the beautiful butterflies
That flutter where the runnel flies!
Silverly glistening over stones
Where yonder nightingale intones
Where he flutes the livelong day
Learning the water's liquid lay;
A lovelier rendering is heard
Fresh from the genius of a bird;
While emulous water vainly tries
To glisten like the glistening eyes
Of nightingales in vernal leaves,
Where yon rosebower softly heaves:
Soon will their mellifluent strain
Woo the rose to life again!
But surely there are lovelier things
Than these are with their cinnamon wings!
Whose grace hath more compelling spells

Than all mine azure damozels!
For as I lay in my pool one day,
A cloud released a gleam,
And the jewel heart of my home grew gay
With a glorifying beam.
There came a rustle in the trees:
I deemed a silver doe
Would sip the ripple of the breeze
Wandering to and fro;
Listless I watched until he should
Arrive here from the shadowy wood.
   It was no deer; it was a boy
   Assailed and took my heart with joy!
   Stealthily, daintily he came,
   Flooding all my sense with flame.
He was clad in a ruby dress
That clung to his breathing loveliness,
While hose of opalescent silk
Revealed his delicate limbs of milk.
   Shyly, timid as a doe,
   He glanced if aught were near or no,
   Then sought him out a pleasant spot
   With clustering forget-me-not,
   And leisurely upon the brink,
   His jewelled raiment to unlink
   Began; that yielding made a way

For hungering eyes of mine to stray
In his fair bosom, velvet fine
Flushing it warmly as with wine,
Velvet and cambric lingering loth
To leave him, yet to faintness both
With warm white satiate, from whence
Stole overpowering my sense
Smooth boy bosom, whose are twin
Rosebuds in a silky skin.

By slender fingers, where the pale
Moon rises in a rosy nail
Cleared from all the lordly dress,
He shone with native loveliness!
Then pressed the grass with shrinking foot,
Strawberry blooms that promise fruit,
Windflower, violet and moss,
And taller flowers that love the loss
Of all their living gold upon
Those limbs unheeding any one:
And yet anon,
As he long blades of grassy gloss
Perplexed daintily disjoins,
A locust leaps upon his loins!
Now finding near a shelving rock,
Behold! he cowers before the shock;

Yet heated how he longs to lave
His beauty in my cooling wave!
His rounded ivory arms have met
Over locks of glossy jet:
Gracefully curls the form so fair
Now upon my yielding air;
Cleaves my laughter-flashing wave,
Delighted one so soft and suave
To gulf within her glassy grave.
Lo! many a clear aerial bubble
Tells the water-heart's sweet trouble!
He lips the ripple, pants and flushes,
Thrusts out white buoyant limbs, and pushes
With turning palm, a snowy swan
Lavishing his bosom upon
My mantling water in the sun!
Now hath he climbed beside the stone,
With filmy lichen overgrown,
Where small swift globes of water twinkle:
There among the periwinkle
Creeping, sidles with a shoulder
Pressed upon the verdured boulder,
Along a narrow ledge to wet
His shining head within the jet
Of foam that skirts my clear cascade,
Leaning under, half afraid.

All my close clinging vision grew
Over him leaping forth anew;
He dives; he rises; I refrain;
He floats upon the shine again.
Luxuriant he lies afloat,
Half his form and half his throat,
Clear from crystalline that sways
Him gently with alluring haze
Veiling some of him from sight,
Filming less or more of white
Wrist or shoulder, as he moves
Fair on wavering water-groves,
Hearing a long sweet croon of doves,
Flying pansies, butterflies,
Moths aflame with crimson dyes,
Haunt his vague and violet eyes:
Odorous shadow of the trees,
Drowsy with the hum of bees,
Amorous nightingales enkindling
At intervals the air and dwindling,
Slim grey waterfall in plashing,
On my stone the wave in washing,
Sweetest music never ending
Blending, never ending
Lulls him in his water-wending.

Why, boy-lover, tell me why
I was doomed to see thee lie,
I was doomed to see thee die,
Tell me why
Even I
Am singing now thy lullaby!
Hear my water sing thee now
A lullaby!
In thy jasmine throat meander
Tender lines of dimple,
And 'tis haunted where they wander
While the waters wimple,
With a shy blue as from veins,
Where soft throat subsiding wanes
Into billowy bosom dreaming
Faintly of the roses;
Whose dim dream a bud discloses
In the gleaming
Undulating almond skin,
Roses nascent soft therein.
Ah! the quiet music of thy beauties un-
　　dulating;
Ah! to feel, to feel, thy gentle warmth of
　　bosom palpitating:
What breath from heaven was breathing
　　behind the fairy flower,

Whose ample one white petal thy body had
    for dower,
Blowing so unerringly to mould thee as
    thou art,
Even so waving waist and limb, and the
    snow about thy heart?
And, if my hands were ne'er to thrill, my
    beautiful, my boy
As they filled them with thy bosom, the
    treasure and the joy,
Why along the ideal limit heaved thy delicate
    form,
So, nor any otherwise, languid, white and
    warm?

      I flung me round him,
      I drew him under:
      I clung, I drowned him,
      My own white wonder! . .

      Father and mother
      Weeping and wild
      Came to the forest,
      Calling the child,
      Came from the palace
      Down to the pool,

Calling my darling,
My beautiful!

Under the water,
Cold and so pale!
Could it be love made
Beauty to fail?
Ah! me for mortals:
In a few moons,
If I had left him,
After some Junes
He would have faded
Faded away,
He the young monarch, whom
All would obey,
Fairer than day;
Alien to spring-time,
Joyless and grey,
He would have faded,
Faded away,
Moving a mockery,
Scorned of the day!
Now I have taken him
All in his prime,
Saved from slow poisoning
Pitiless Time,

Filled with his happiness,
One with the prime,
Saved from the cruel
Dishonour of Time.
Laid him, my beautiful,
Laid him to rest
Loving adorable,
Softly to rest
Here in my crystalline,
Here in my breast!

A VISION OF THE DESERT

METHOUGHT I saw the morning bloom
A solemn wilderness illume,
Desert sand and empty air:
Yet in a moment I was aware
Of One who grew from forth the East,
Mounted upon a vasty Beast
It swung with silent equal stride,
With a mighty shadow by the side:
The tawny tufted hair was frayed;
The long protruding snout was laid
Level before it; looking calm away
From that imperial rising of the Day.
Methought a very awful One
Towered speechless thereupon:
All the figure like a cloud
An ample mantle did enshroud,
Folding heavily dark and white,
Concealing all the face from sight,

Save where through storm-like rifts there came
A terrible gleam of eyes like flame.

Then I beheld how on his arm
A child was lying without alarm.
With innocent rest it lay asleep;
Awakening soon to laugh and leap;
Yet well I knew, whatever passed,
The arm that held would hold it fast.
Nor ever then it sought to know
Whose tender strength encircled so,
Living incuriously wise
Under the terrible flame of eyes.
In those sweet early morning hours
It played with dewy wreathing flowers,
Drinking oft from a little flask
Under the mantle: I heard it ask:
Yea, and at other times the cooling cup
Gentle and merciful He tilted up.

But when the sun began to burn,
I saw the child more restless turn,
Seeking to view the silent One:
Then, growing graver thereupon,
It whispered " Father!" but I never heard
If any lips in answer stirred.

Yet if no answer reached the child,
I know not why he lay and smiled,
Raising his little arms on high
In a solemn rapture quietly!

The shadow moved, and growing less,
A blue blaze ruled the wilderness.
The child alert with life and fire
Gazed all around with infinite desire.
Erect he sat, contented now no more
To nestle and feed upon the homely store:
He searched the lessening distance whence
    they came
He peered into the clear cærulean flame
His hand would mingle with the shaggy
    hair
Of that enormous Living Thing which bare,
Whose feet were planted in the powdery
    ground
With ne'er a pause, with ne'er a sound.
Yon fascinating, wondrous Infinite
His clear young eyes explored with keen
    delight:
He gazed into the muffled Countenance
Undazzled with the rifted radiance:
Then giving names to all that he espied,

He murmured with a bright triumphant pride,
"I hold their secret: lo! I am satisfied."
Oh! it was rare to see the lovely child,
As with a gaze ecstatical he smiled,
Following with eager, splendour-beaming
    eyes
A bird magnificent who sailed the skies
On vast expanded plumes of sanguine white,
Enamoured of transcendant azure light,
Higher and higher soaring to the sun;
Claiming a share in his dominion;
Elate with ardour, like unwearying youth,
Imperially at home in awful realms of Truth!

But ah! the sun beat fierce and merciless
Upon the boundless, barren wilderness,
Then soon, responsive to a slakeless thirst,
Behold upon his ravished sight there burst
A vision of a far off lake most fair,
Where many a palm was dallying with air,
And soft mimosa: how alluringly
Smiled the sweet water in a blinding sky!
Can he not hear a gentle turtle coo
Among light leaves, yea, very wavelets blue
Lapping among green reeds upon the shore,
Calling him to abide for evermore?

Ah! how doth he impetuous entreat,
And chide the silent, never-lingering feet!
Yet was it strange, for as the feet advanced
The lake receded and the waters danced
An eerie dance with all the belts of trees,
And mingled with them till the sand with these
On the horizon made a marge that wavered
And all blew sidelong, thin white flame that
    quavered—
Then one low whispered,—" 'Tis the Devil's
    water !"
While in his ear there pealed cruel un-
    earthly laughter.
On this the child fell ill with fever,
Made many a vain yet wild endeavour
To fling himself from forth the grasp
That held with ne'er relaxing clasp,
Murmuring, " None holds me fast;
I am a plaything of the blast."
But the Rider from the girdled store
Ministered to him as before.

And while the shadow veered by stealth,
A measure of his primal health
The boy resumed : an air that fanned
Blew veritably o'er the sand;

And little birds before them flew
Vested in a sober hue,
A paly brown, to suit the home
Where 'tis their destiny to roam.
Yet I am sure that ne'er a bird
Fluting more soft and sweet was heard
Among the lawns of Paradise,
Than these in such a humble guise,
Who, without any rest or haste
Travel warbling o'er the waste.
Moreover in the sterile soil
Some spots of verdure, while the travellers toil,
Arise; yea, even the sweet oases
That vanished with the feigning, undulating
    graces,
Were fair and real delight, however fleeing,
With law distinct of transitory being;
Only illusion for deluding eyes,
That yearn for what nor waste nor world
    supplies
Some dim ideal of the soul,
That ever loves and grows toward the
    illimitable whole.

But ever as they two solitary range,
And as the immeasurable horizons change,

Upon the child more burdensome doth lie
Sense of impenetrable mystery.
Erst he imagined that he chose to go;
But now he feels, whether he will or no
One carries him: he joyed to be in life
For possibilities of boundless strife,
Wresting resplendent secrets bold from all:
Now the unmasked immensities appal,
Weighing incumbent on the sense and
     thought,
As on a dwindling grain of dust, as on a
     thing of nought!
A moment looking toward the shrouded Face
Now is he fain his timid eyes to abase:
"Father, unveil!" he tremulously cries,
Fearing he asks impossibilities.

     Yet hearken! voices musical
Like dew upon the desert fall,
Rising and falling,
Calling, calling!
Very plaintive, sweet and low,
As the lonely pilgrims go:
Are they spirits of the wild,
Calling, answering low and mild?
Is it a voice of one departed,

Plaining gentle, unquiet-hearted,
Vainly hungering to enfold
His beloved as of old?   .
Severed from our living kind,
In a feeble wandering wind
Wandering ever? none can tell
Whence the mystic murmurs well:
But oft an Arab roaming far
Over sands of Sahara
Hears the sweet mysterious measure
With a solemn-hearted pleasure,
Saying, " No wind among the stones
Breathes the rare unearthly tones! "
And howsoe'er it be they tell
The soul of things ineffable,
Of a life beyond our death or birth,
Of a universe beyond the earth!
Monotonously weary seemed the way,
While light declining faded slowly away
Some haze obscured a gradual westering sun
And all the oppressive firmament was wan.
In it voluminous appears to form
From the horizon a continent of storm,
A ponderous bulk of gathering indigo,
Tinged in its formidable overflow
With hues of livid purple poison flowers.

In ghastlier whiteness for the night that
    lowers
Strewing forlorn the desolate desert pale,
Some grinning skeletons of men assail
My vision; while a monstrous bird of prey
From a putrescent corpse rends fierce away
The clinging flesh with horrid sound of
    tearing,
Its beak abruptly, pulling, baring;
Bald-headed, hideous neck low crouched
    betwixt
The pressure of strong talons curved, infixed:
Now the proud brain, like fearful Madness
    mangling,
Like Sin now with the reeking bosom
    wrangling:
Like ignorance, disease, war, tyranny, star-
    vation,
Eating the vitals of a noble fallen nation!
This creature, as they pass, a moment glaring
Voracious-eyed, with vasty vans that cover
A little further on obscene doth hover
A grey hyena, and he laughs a peal
Of beastly laughter, scraping up a meal
Loathsome from forth the sand: there is a
    howl

Dolefully borne from where the lean wolves
   prowl!
Then silence falls upon the deepening gloom,
And sultry air forebodes the smothering
   Simoom.
Looking towards the child with deep dismay,
I noticed his fair ringlets turned to grey,
And sparse like withered bents upon his
   head:
His pale, worn countenance was drawn with
   dread;
Yet in his eyes there burned a grand resolve,
No sights of terror lightly might dissolve.
And now I heard him murmur, "Mighty
   Father!
I trust thee; yea, to thee I cling the rather,
Albeit I may not see thine awful face!"
Then I was sure he felt the strong embrace
Tighten around him, though a Skeleton
Came stalking from the night to lead them on:
A far-off murmur swelled into a wildering
   roar;
A hurricane of flame and sand whirled like
   a conqueror!
And when the o'erwhelming terrible death-
   tempest on them broke,

The shrinking child crept nestling close
under the Father's cloak.

Then darkness swallowed the portentous
plain.
When faint it dawned upon my eyes again,
Lo! there was moonlight in a sky serene;
All lay at peace beneath the melancholy
sheen.
No voice was heard, no living thing was
seen.
Yet ere I was aware, that awful Apparition
Once more emerged upon my mortal vision—
The shrouded, dim, unutterable Form,
With eyes that flame as through the rifts
of storm,
Mounted on that colossal Living Thing,
Bearing the child now softly slumbering—
While all confused immeasurable shadow
fling.
Peacefully lay the boy's pale silent head:
And looking long, I knew that he was dead.
Then all my wildered anguish forced a way
Through my wild lips: "Reveal, O lord, I
pray,
Whither thou carriest him!" I cried aloud:

No voice responded from the shadowy shroud;
Only methought that something like a hand
Was raised to point athwart the shadowy
　　land;
And while afar the dwindling twain were
　　borne,
I, gazing all around with eyes forlorn,
Divined the bloom of some unearthly morn!

Where was he carried? to an isle of calm,
Lulled with sweet water and the pensile
　　palm?
Vanishing havens on the pilgrimage
Surely some more abiding home presage!
Or must the Sire attain always alone
The happy Land with never a living son?

O! awful, silent, everlasting One!
If thou must roam those islands of the west.
Ever with some dead child upon thy breast,
Who would have hailed the glory being blest,
Eternity were one long moan for rest!
For do we not behold thee morn by morn,
Issuing from the East with one new-born,
Carrying him silently, none knoweth whither,
Knowing only all we travel swiftly thither.

SUSPIRIA

Lines addressed to H. F. B.

Do you remember the billowy roar of tu-
multuous ocean
Darkling, emerald, eager under vaults of
the cave
Shattered to simmer of foam on a boulder
of delicate lilac
Disenchantless youth of the clear immortal
wave?   .
Labyrinths begemmed with fairy lives of
the water,
Sea-sounding palace halls far statelier than
a King's
Seethe of illumined floor with a never wea-
rying motion,
Oozy enchased live walls where a sea-
music rings?

Do you remember the battle our brown-
  winged arrowy vessel
  Waged with wind and tide, a foaming
  billowy night,
To a sound as of minute guns, when gloomy
  hearts of the hollows
  With sullen pride rebuffed invading
  Ocean's might?

Do you remember the Altarlet towers that
  front the Cathedral
  Dark and scarred sheer crag, flashed o'er
  by the wild sea-mews?
How they wheel aloft lamenting, souls of
  the ululant tempest!
  And the lightning billows clash in the
  welter Odin brews!

A sinister livid glare from under brows of
  the storm-Sun!
  Brows of piled-up cloud, threatening grim
  Brechou,
Bleaching to ghastly pale the turbulent
  trouble of water,
  While the ineffable burden of grey world
  o'er me grew!

Yea, all the weary waste of cloud confused
    with the ocean
  Fell full-charged with Doom on a founder-
    ing human heart;
Our souls were moved asunder, away to an
    infinite distance,
  While all the love that warmed me waned
    and will depart.
Fiends of the whirlwind howl for a wild
    carousal of slaughter
  Of all that is holy and fair, so shrills the
    demon wail;
Ruin of love and youth with all we have
    deemed immortal!
  My child lies dead in the dark, and I
    begin to fail!
Wonderful visions wane, tall towers of phan-
    tasy tumble;
  I shrink from the frown without me, there
    is no smile within
I cower by the fireless hearth of an un-
    inhabited chamber.
Alone with Desolation and the dumb ghost
    of my sin.

I have conversed with the aged; once their
    souls were a furnace
Now they are gleams in mouldered vaults
    of the memory:
All the long sound of the Human wanes to
    wails of a shipwreck,
    Drowned in the terrible roar of violent
    sons of the sea!
    In the immense storm-chaunt of winds
    waves of the sea!
And if we have won some way in our weary
    toil to the summit
    Do we not slidder ever back to the mouth
    of the pit?
When I behold the random doom that en-
    gulfs the creature,
    I wonder is the irony of God perchance
    in it?
'Tis a hideous spectacle to shake the sides
    off fiends with laughter
    Where in the amphitheatre of our red
    world they sit!
Yea, and the rosiest Love in a songful
    heart of a lover,
    Child of Affinity, Joy, Occasion, beautiful
    May,

May sour to a wrinkled Hate, may wear
and wane to Indifference
Ah! Love, an ' thou be mortal, all will
soon go grey!
O when our all on earth is wrecked on
reefs of disaster,
May the loud Night that whelms be found
indeed God's Day!

Our aims but half our own, we are drifted
hither and thither
The quarry so fiercely hunted rests un-
heeded now;
And if we seized our bauble, it is fallen
into ashes,
But a fresh illusion haunts the ever aching
brow,
Is the world a welter of dream, with ne'er
an end nor an issue,
Or doth One weave Dark Night, with
Morning's golden strand,
To a Harmony with sure hand?
Ah! for a vision of God! for a mighty grasp
of the real,
Feet firm based on granite in place of
crumbling sand!

O to be face to face, and heart to heart
    with our dearest,
  Lost in mortal mists of the unrevealing
    land!
Oh! were we disenthralled from casual moods
    of the outward,
  Slaves to the smile or frown of tyrant,
    mutable Time!
Might we abide unmoved in central deeps
    of the Spirit,
  Where the mystic jewel Calm glows ever-
    more sublime!
The dizzying shows of the world that fall
    and tumble to chaos,
  Dwell irradiate there in everlasting prime.
But the innermost spirit of man who is
    one with the Universal,
  Yearns to exhaust, to prove, the Immense
    of Experience,
Explores, recedes, makes way, distils a food
    from a poison,
  From strife with Death wrings power,
    and seasoned confidence
O'er the awakening infant, drowsing eld
    and the mindless,

Their individual Spirit glows enthroned
    in Heaven,
Albeit at dawn or even or from confusion
    of cloudland,
    Earth of their full radiance may remain
      bereaven:
    Yea, under God's grand eyes all souls lie
      pure and shriven.

    Nay! friend beloved! remember purple
      robes of the cavern,
And all the wonderful dyes in dusky
    halls of the sea,
When a lucid lapse of the water lent thrills
    of exquisite pleasure,
    A tangle of living lights all over us
    tenderly,
When our stilly bark lay floating, or we
    were lipping the water
    Breast to breast with the glowing, ardent
      heart of the deep
That was a lovelier hour, whispering hope
    to the spirit,
    Breathing a halcyon calm, that lulled
    despair to sleep;

Fairy flowers of the ocean, opening inner-
much wonder,
Kindle a rosy morn impearled in the
waterways,
A myriad tiny diamond founts arise in the
coralline,
Anemones love to be laved in the life of
the chrysoprase
The happy heart of the water in many unknown recesses
Childly babbled, and freely to glad companions:
We will be patient, friend, through all the
moods of the terror
Waiting in solemn hope resurrection of
our suns!

Cherish loves that are left, pathetic stars
in the gloaming;
Howe'er they may wax and wane, they
are with us to the end,
The Past is all secure, the happy hours and
the mournful
Involved i' the very truth of God Himself,
my friend!

It is well to wait in the darkness for the
　　Deliverer's moment,
　With a hand in the hand of God, strong
　　Sire of the Universe;
It is well to work our work, with cheering
　　tones for a brother
　Whose poor bowed soul, like ours, the
　　horrible gulfs immerse;
Then dare all gods to the battle! Who of
　　them all may shame us?
　The very shows of the world have fleeting
　　form from thee:
Discover but thy task, embrace it firm with
　　a purpose;
　Find, and hold by Love, for Love is
　　Eternity,

Sark, 1881.

O to be sure for ever! weary of hopes
　　and guesses,
　I would the film might fall that veils our
　　orbs in night!
At eve grey phantom armies guard the
　　mighty mountain,
　Denying free approach to wistful wonder-
　　ing sight:

A Presence dim divined through blind, impal-
pable motion,
An awful formless Form, i' the core of
change unmoved,
No more was ours, until the grand invin-
cible Angel
The clear-eyed North blew bare Heaven's
azure heights and proved
Hope's heavenliest flight weak-winged; his
breath with clamorous challenge
Dissolved the cloud-battalions, withering
shamed away:
Behold in sunrise dyed, a wondrous vision
of high crag,
Spires of leaping flame arrested in mid-
play;
Peak, rock-tower and dome; huge peals of
an ocean of thunder
Assumed a bodily form in yonder wild
array!
And the long continuous roll of cloudy storm
subsiding
Was tranced to awful slopes of smooth
grey precipice,
While over all up-soared, retiring into the
heavens,

Ever higher and higher, snows and gleam-
    ing ice!
Plain beyond plain, the strophes of a glori-
    ous poem,
    Voyaging stately and calm to heights of
    the argument. . . .
How to be sure for ever? deepening all our
    being,
    And emptying self of self, with Truth we
    shall be blent.

Yon hierarchy sublime of calm ethereal
    mountain
Was born of earth's fierce passion, world-
    confounding throes
Fire and battle and gloom; the livid demon
    of lightning
    Flashed his zigzag blaze to be a norm
    for those;
Birth and death, monotonous toil in deeps
    of the ocean,
    Co-operant blind to fashion a far-off repose.
Whose brief earth-hour may taste ripe future
    fruit of the ages?
    Guage with a life's one pace the march
    of the armies of God?

Forestall results of time, flash all the sun
    from a dew-drop?
But where the Sire hath willed, there
    every footstep trod.

'Tis only a little we know; but ah! the
    Saviour knoweth;
I will lay the head of a passionate child
    on His gentle broest,
I poured out with the wave, He founded
    firm with the mountain;
In the calm of His infinite eyes I have
    sought and found my rest.
O to be still on the heart of the God we
    know in the Saviour,
Feeling Him more than all the noblest
    gifts He gave!
To be is more than to know, we near the
    Holy of Holies
In coming home to Love; we shall know
    beyond the grave.

Ah! the peace of the beautiful realm,
    like dew, sinks into my spirit;
True and tender friend, I love to be here
    with thee.

The pines, tall fragrant columns of a magnificent temple,
Are ranged before the ethereal mountain
majesty;
While a dove-coloured lapse of the water
merrily murmurs a confidence
Into a quiet ear of twilit beautiful bowers;
Sweet breath of the pyrola woos us, white
waxen elf of the woodland,
And two tired hearts may play awhile
with the innocent flowers.

San Martino 1882.

WILD LOVE ON THE SEA

" O SING to me, sing to me, foam of the
    Sea,
Sing while we sail, to my darling and me,
While we heel to the wind, the foam flies
    from the bow,
My love laughs, we were never so happy
    as now!

We rush through the water, we scatter the
    spray,
The foam-bubbles leap in the blue light away,
My sails are less white than your bosom or
    hand,
We will sail on for ever afar from the land.

O dotards may mumble their winterly talk,
But the young joy of living their age may
    not baulk,

We shall soon be beyond their bleak Northerly
  Clime,
Who fain would persuade us that love is a
  crime.

Never fear, never fear, nestle closer to me,
O we joy to bound over wild waves and be
  free!
For our bridal sing, winds! and blithe billows,
  your song
Breathe into your clarion loudly and long!

Winds whistle and fill the full-bellying sail;
Yea, what if they rise and blow shrill to a
  gale?
My boat is a rare one, she swims like a bird—
Ha! what if the roar on the reefs may be
  heard?

You're the loveliest lady that ever was known,
My rival I slew, and my bride is my own;
Warm bosom to bosom, hot mouth unto mouth,
We are flying to lovelier lands of the
  South . . . ."

" Nay the sky's growing darker, I fain would
  return—"

" Your doubts are too late, love, your scruples
    I spurn ; "
" I fear thee, I fear thee, fierce lover of mine ;
" Thy lips are the wild wave, thy breasts
    are the brine ! "

" Ho ! with storm to the windward, and
    breakers to lee,
" They go swimming with Death, who go
    sailing with me ! "

NOCTURNE

At the close of a day in December
I went by the winter sea,
And my soul was a fading ember
In abysms of immensity.

Then God spake out of the gloaming
Where the wave gave over strife,
And fell, wan, feeble, and foaming,
'Man what hast thou done with life?'

I was ware of a mournful throbbing,
Of a sea-pulse on the shore,
And I heard in it women sobbing,
Whom I loved and who loved me of yore.

In a rift of the cloudy distance
Lay blood from the fallen sun,

While the wind with a low insistance,
Like a breaking heart moaned on.

O blithely the sun ascended
With carol of bird and breeze!
And now, his career being ended,
He fell through the leafless trees,
Amid sighing sounds of seas.

Do the life and the work fail wholly
For a man who hath lived and loved?
Through the joy and the melancholy
With finishing hand God moved,

"AH! LOVE YE ONE ANOTHER WELL!"

Ah! love ye one another well,
For the hour will come
When one of you is lying dumb;
Ye would give worlds then for a word,
That never may be heard;
Ye would give worlds then for a glance
That may be yours by ne'er a chance;
Ah! love ye one another well!

For if ye wrung a tear
Like molten iron it will sear;
The look that proved you were unkind
With hot remorse will be blind;
And though you pray to be forgiven,
How will ye know that ye are shriven?
Ah! love ye one another well!

198